FIXER

A BAD BOY ROMANCE

SAMANTHA WESTLAKE

Copyright © 2016 Samantha Westlake

All rights reserved.

ISBN:1537714082
ISBN-13:9781537714080

DEDICATION

For all my readers, both new and returning.
I write it for you.

CHAPTER ONE

Striding into the club, brilliant spotlights and the flashes of camera phones going off all around him, the man didn't bother to straighten his jacket or check his tie. He didn't look down as his polished black shoes strode ahead, didn't brush any microscopic bits of dust off of his broad shoulders or dark pants.

This man knew that he looked good. No, scratch that - he looked amazing. The suit was worth every penny of the nearly five thousand dollars that he'd paid for it; he felt it clinging perfectly to his muscular body in all the right places.

Even in a club like this one, he knew that his suit, shoes, even the Cartier Astrotourbillon watch gleaming on his wrist, all attracted plenty of attention. The young women who hung around in places like this could gauge the net worth of a man down to the penny, and their eyes lingered hungrily on his powerful frame as he passed.

He didn't glance over at them, didn't allow for eye contact to even offer up the suggestion of something happening. Not tonight.

Keegan Tanner was here on business.

Still, he knew how to give the right impression. In a town like this one, after all, everyone had an agenda, and deceit was second nature to Tanner, just like it was for everyone else that he knew. So instead of searching the crowded club for his target, he headed for the bar.

There was a space open for him, of course. Tanner didn't need to deal with pushing his way in past a crowd of jocks and bros all milling about and taking shots. He was better than that. He was the kind of person, he thought to himself with a little grin that he couldn't completely hide, who made things happen.

The bartender popped up next to him immediately. Tanner's suit wasn't flashy, but its cut and fine fabric practically screamed money - and the heavy Cartier on his wrist acted like a bullhorn for that scream.

"What can I get you?" he asked.

Tanner didn't bother asking for a menu. "Laphroaig twenty-five, neat."

The expensive order didn't faze the man behind the counter. Less than thirty seconds later, a glass with two fingers of beautiful amber liquid was set carefully in front of him.

Instead of a credit card, Tanner pulled a hundred dollar bill from his pocket, dropping it on the bar. He didn't want to leave any trace that he'd been here, and using a credit card was an easy way to be connected with an event. He knew better than to make that mistake.

Sweeping up the glass, Tanner held it first before his nose, taking in the complex aroma and bouquet of the scotch before allowing the liquid to reach his lips. Stepping back, towards the wall, he let his eyes drift around the interior of the club.

Billy Martin's usually cultivated a more reserved atmosphere during the dinnertime hours, but this late at night, the place opened up into a party zone, albeit a high-end and expensive one. In addition, the latest

Congressional session had just reconvened, and staffers and congressmen alike were still energized from vacation and looking to make new connections.

Several girls slipped past Tanner, giggling as their tiny dresses and slutty outfits threatened to reveal both nipples and asses. Tanner's eyes strayed for a moment to follow them, but he pulled his gaze off of the girls with an effort.

He had a job to do here; he could enjoy a bit of fun after he'd completed his assignment.

Tanner recognized several faces in the crowd, both male and female, but he didn't see his target. He frowned, covering his irritation with another sip of the liquor, letting the burn flow down his throat.

His target must be in the raised dais area. A slightly more exclusive section of the restaurant, although still not any problem for Tanner. Holding his glass in one hand, he cut across the dance floor, slipping sideways to move between some of the gyrating bodies. Hands reached out to brush against him, feeling him up, but he didn't push them away. Instead, he just slid on, letting the hands drop off of the smooth fabric of his suit.

Although, now that he considered his challenge…

The girls who'd smiled and giggled at him a few minutes earlier now danced nearby, their hands up above their heads and gyrating perfect, lithe little teenage bodies back and forth in the flickering lights. One of them, the blonde, turned and looked back over her shoulder at Tanner. She bit her lip in a way that, if Tanner wasn't on a mission, would likely have promised an unforgettable rest of his night.

He smiled back, raising a hand and crooking a finger at them.

The blonde didn't move; she just raised her eyebrows as if to ask, "so what? What are you offering?"

In answer, Tanner flicked his eyes towards the dais, the VIP area.

That sealed it. The blonde smiled, turning and giving her chest one last little bounce to make her perky tits wiggle in a manner that pulled at his eyes like a magnet. She nudged her two companions, and they headed over to Tanner.

Looping his arm over the blonde, Tanner turned and headed for the raised part of the restaurant.

The massive bouncer standing at the entrance to the raised dais area looked like he'd been poured into his suit. Tanner cast a dismissive eye over the cheap fabric, but he didn't miss how the suit strained to cover the bouncer's huge arms and shoulders. This wasn't a man to cross, not if Tanner didn't want to be thrown - airborne - out of the club.

"Name?" he grunted at Tanner, his little black eyes squinting.

"Keegan Tanner." Tanner waited a beat, trying to hide his irritation as the bouncer consulted a list. A paper list, for chrissake! Who still used something like that? Instead, he flicked his attention down to the squirming little blonde pressing herself against him. She knew exactly what kind of reaction her movements provoked, he knew, as she smirked up at him like a vixen.

"Need me to spell it for you?" he asked sarcastically, as the bouncer's huge, stubby finger slowly slid down the sheet of paper on the clipboard.

"Nah, found it. 'Kay, you're good." Predictably, Billy Martin's had hired the bouncer more for his muscles than for any sort of cognitive ability.

Tanner slid past the bouncer, the girls flouncing along with him, stepping up onto the raised area. Up here, gauzy curtains helped create the illusion of privacy, blocking a little of the booming sound from the massive speakers on the dance floor. The area was broken up by couches and low tables, turning a large space into lots of intimate little areas where half a dozen people could relax, sip at drinks, and talk without needing to shout over the pounding music.

Tanner's eyes swept around the area as he paused, idly letting his hand slide down the blonde's backside. There! He spotted the unmistakable white hair of his target, sitting in a booth several rows over. Tanner cut towards the man, sliding into a booth several spots away that nonetheless offered a clear line of sight.

"So, girls," he murmured to the three young women who bounced into the booth along with him. "Want to have some fun?"

"We like fun," the blonde replied eagerly, her two friends nodding along like puppets. "What sort of fun?"

Tanner guessed that the sparkle in her eyes wasn't entirely natural. She probably got a bit of help from some "natural enhancers," the kind that came as a white powder and went up her nose. "Not that kind of fun," he replied, and saw her face droop slightly in a momentary frown. "But one that will pay off well for you." His eyes moved to her two companions. "All of you."

He saw interest in the girls' eyes, so he kept talking. "See that man over there?" He pointed to his target. "The one with the white hair, in the blue suit? He's a senator - and a buddy of mine. Senator Waltz. And although he'll never admit it, he's lonely."

"Aww, that's so sad," commented one of the brunettes, not sounding sympathetic at all. Instead, she already sounded hungry. Tanner swallowed his grin.

This was going to be too easy.

"It is. His wife's a complete bitch, has no respect for his job. He does a lot of work to help the people from his state, and no one ever appreciates him for it." He noticed a waitress passing by, and waved her over. "A bottle of Dom, and four glasses - three for my companions, here-" the girls giggled, "-and one for their guest."

As the waitress hurried off to retrieve his order, Tanner turned to the girls. "So? Can you go and cheer up my buddy, the senator?"

The two brunettes looked ready to hop over to Waltz's booth right away, but the blonde's eyes remained on Tanner. "And I was hoping that you'd be the one partying with us," she purred.

He smiled back at her, beckoning her forward - and from his pocket, he drew out a business card. "Entertain my buddy for tonight, and I'll be happy to thank you whenever you next feel like… partying," he offered, passing the card over to her.

The blonde made the card disappear, although given her skimpy little outfit, Tanner wasn't sure where she managed to secret it away. "Deal," she said, just as the waitress reappeared with the champagne and glasses.

Smiling, Tanner leaned back in the booth, sipping at his scotch as he watched the girls bounce over to Senator Waltz's booth. He looked surprised and opened his mouth to protest at first, but the blonde leaned forward to dangle her breasts in his face, cutting off his complaints. Tanner nearly snorted into his glass.

So easy.

The waitress handed over the champagne, and the blonde tossed back the entire contents of her glass in a single swallow. Her eyes flicked briefly over to Tanner before returning back to Waltz, making sure that he saw her open up her throat.

Waltz didn't miss the implications, either. His hand curled out around the girl, and she snuggled in against him, her hands already straying to dangerous areas. Tanner watched for a moment longer, making sure that Waltz wasn't suddenly about to grow a conscience - and then reached into the inner jacket pocket of his suit.

Drawing out a small but powerful camera, he snapped several shots, varying several settings to make sure that he captured every angle of the senator's features. At one point, Tanner even leaned a little bit out of his booth, holding out the camera so he could capture the blonde's hand as it rested firmly on the man's crotch.

Snapping the pictures only took a few moments. "Just like that," Tanner murmured to himself, stowing the camera away. "Easy."

Of course, these pictures would likely never see the light of day. Tomorrow, as Senator Waltz recovered from his hangover, Tanner would pay a surreptitious visit to his office. With just the two of them alone in the office, he'd bring out a few chosen images from the album, spread a couple of glossy, high-resolution prints out on the senator's desk. He'd let the man mull over these images for a few minutes, letting the desperation grow.

And then…

Well, some of the Pentagon defense contracts were up for renewal - and Senator David Waltz sat on the Subcommittee on Financial and Contracting Oversight. Although the senator was known for taking more of a dove stance, rather than a hawk stance, on military spending, Tanner suspected that he might change his mind, especially after seeing these pictures.

After all, Senator Waltz built much of his Senate career on his integrity. Wouldn't it be a shame if that integrity was compromised by some very illicit pictures surfacing at the absolute worst time, appearing on the front pages of several newspapers and all over the web?

Sitting back in his booth, Tanner let himself smile, his lips pulling back to reveal perfect white teeth. He savored the last of his Laphroaig, considered ordering another.

In fact, he did want another.

He checked out the waitress's ass as she sauntered away with his empty glass, promising to bring him a refill. Not bad. If the blonde ended up going home with the Senator after all, he had plenty of other options.

Yes, Tanner thought to himself, he had everything a man could want. Wealth, power, women drooling over him… all of it was second nature.

And moving among them, like a shark amid tuna… all in a day's work.

CHAPTER TWO

The next afternoon, Keegan Tanner strode across the National Mall, breezing along and doing his best to not notice the occasional crowd of milling, gawking tourists. Amateurs, he thought to himself with disdain. Coming here, staring wildly at the monuments and snapping photographs of sculptures, as if that was where the power lay.

Tanner knew that the monuments, the big buildings and fancy galleries full of oil paintings, were just window dressing. That wasn't where the real power lay, the true shot callers in Washington, DC.

He stepped off of the main avenue and headed up the broad stone steps to a nondescript, blocky building, on First Street, a few blocks away from the white dome of the Capitol. He ducked into the lobby, glad to feel the cold wash of air conditioned air hit him and sweep away the thin layer of sweat starting to break out on his forehead. Summer in DC tended to hang around into the fall, as if reluctant to relinquish its stranglehold on the city.

"ID, Mr. Tanner?"

Tanner sighed at the guard. "Come on, Charlie, I'm just here to drop off an envelope for Pribus. Do I really need to dig the damn card out every time?"

The guard shrugged, not without some sympathy in his expression. "Hey, rules are rules. Gotta keep this place secure. More than my ass is worth, if someone gets in here." He chuckled. "You know the secrets that we keep in this place, more than anyone."

"I do know, I suppose," Tanner acknowledged. He reached into his jacket pocket and withdrew his ID card, which he held out for Charlie to scan.

"Thank you, sir," Charlie said a moment later, after the scanner beeped and flashed green. "Sounds like things went well?"

"Quite well, yes." Tanner started to head past the guard, but then paused. What the hell, Charlie could use a bit of excitement in his life. Poor sucker was stuck standing at this desk all day, getting paid squat. "Here, you want to see what we're up against?"

Ducking back to the guard's station, Tanner pulled open the large yellow-brown envelope in his hands. He tugged out a few of the photographs he'd chosen to print off, fanning them out so that Charlie could see.

"Damn!" Charlie whistled, his eyes going wide as he leaned in to peer closer at a few of the images. "Is that-"

"Our frequent enemy, scourge of the Republican party, David Waltz," Tanner finished for him. "The last bastion of morality in Washington, speaking out against corruption and lies." He chuckled. "And no, that's definitely not his wife. Neither of them, in fact."

Charlie shook his head in mingled shock and amusement as Tanner slipped the pictures back into the envelope. "You do it again, Mr. Tanner. Best fixer in Washington, you are."

"And don't let anyone tell you otherwise," Tanner said. He made a show of glancing at his watch. "Actually,

Charlie, I'm running a bit late for another appointment." He hefted the envelope. "You think that you could…"

"No problem, sir," the guard jumped in. He reached out and took the envelope from Tanner. "I'll have it right up to Mr. Pribus's office."

"No rush on them," Tanner added, giving Charlie a wink. He could see that the guard was itching to fish out the photos and get a second, longer look - probably in private. "Waltz already agreed to make sure that nobody at the Pentagon goes home disappointed that their contract's been dropped. These are just some extra insurance."

Charlie reassured Tanner once again that he could handle dropping off the pictures, and Tanner believed him. He'd trusted Charlie with other jobs before, and knew that the guard wouldn't let him down.

With a wave, Tanner headed out of the Republican Party's national headquarters. Capitol Lounge, his destination, was only a few blocks away, and Tanner made a spur of the moment decision to walk, rather than catch a taxi or Uber ride. His long legs made short work of the distance, and he relished the opportunity to check his reflection in some of the glass storefront windows he passed.

Before ducking into the Capitol Lounge, he stopped at one of these reflecting windows, raising a hand to his hair. Of course, not a single dark strand was out of place. Barely out of his twenties, and getting more handsome by the day, Tanner grinned to himself. On the top of his obvious good looks, he was also at the top of his career, with half of the most powerful people in DC on his speed dial.

Despite the sun sitting low in the sky, the heat still settled over the city like an oppressive wet blanket. Tanner grabbed the door to the Capitol Lounge and slipped inside before he could start sweating through his expensive suit.

"Hey, Keegan! Over here!"

The interior of the Capitol Lounge was decked out in

dark wood, with a wood-paneled ceiling and a long bar running almost the entire length of the Nixon Room. The bar was only sparsely populated at the moment, although Tanner knew that it would fill up quickly as the sun dropped below the horizon and staffers across the city managed to escape from the watchful eyes of their bosses.

At the bar, a lone man waved his slightly chubby hand in the air, as if Tanner could somehow miss spotting him. "Yo, Keegan!" he called out again.

Tanner rolled his eyes as he crossed the interior of the Nixon Room, over to the bar. "Yes, Freddie, I see you. Everyone sees you. You don't need to shout."

"I just wanted to make sure that I got your attention," Freddie pouted, as Tanner pulled out the stool beside him and took a seat. His pout turned to a smirk. "You know, since you walk around with your head up your ass most of the time."

"Big words, coming from a guy who hasn't touched a girl since his mom stopped breastfeeding," Tanner fired back.

"Not true! I also worked at a senior citizen's center for a year after college, doing IT work for them." Freddie's eyes grew misty as he gazed off into the distance. "Oh, Mrs. Constance, the way your bosom pressed against me whenever you tried to show me pictures of your grandchildren…"

"You're disgusting," Tanner said, laughing as he socked Freddie in the arm.

"Right back at you," his chubby drinking companion replied. "I'm just glad to see that you haven't dropped dead from one of the half dozen venereal diseases fighting for control of your body! Or is it up to a full dozen different strains, now?"

"After last night? Probably closer to two dozen."

Freddie's eyes went wide. "Okay, you need to tell me everything."

"What, so you can live vicariously through me?"

"Uh, duh." Freddie turned towards Tanner, spreading his arms wide. "I mean, look at the two of us! You're a... What's the term for your job, again?"

"Lobbying specialist," Tanner supplied.

"Fixer," Freddie said. "A high-powered Republican fixer, walking around in your fancy three thousand dollar suits-"

"Five thousand."

"-and flashing your exotic, overpriced watch that's worth enough to buy a car-"

"Several cars, really."

"-and with your perfectly sculpted Adonis body and white teeth and amazing hair and wads of money clogging up your pockets!" Freddie paused, frowning. "Okay, hold on. What was my point with all of this, again?"

"I wish I could tell you," Tanner sighed. "Unfortunately, I'm as lost as you." He spotted the bartender, a young woman with dyed platinum hair and a generous expanse of cleavage on display. He gave her a wave, and received a dimpled smile in response.

"Oh, now I remember," Freddie piped up after a moment of watching Tanner smile at the bartender. "My point is that I'm never going to pull as much tail as you, so I want to hear about your exploits so that I can have something to fill the void in my life."

Tanner started to protest, but he knew that Freddie spoke the truth. Maybe if he flashed his last name - Vanderbilt, yes, like the old robber baron from the nineteenth century - he might do a bit better. Not by much, however. Even with the suggestion of family wealth, any girl would still have to deal with Freddie being, well...

...Freddie. No other word for it.

Next to him, Freddie talked right over Tanner's halfhearted protest. "Look, I know that you love bragging about this, even if you deny it to my face. I see the way you grin whenever you've got something juicy. So c'mon, spill!"

Tanner sighed as he turned back to Freddie. "Why do I put up with you, again?"

"Oh, I know this one!" Freddie grinned. "Despite all your good looks and charm, you're a shallow asshole who can't make real friends, so you keep me around in order to act as your confidante! And since I'm chubby and nerdy and in IT, you don't feel threatened by me!"

"Brutal," Tanner winced, but he did have to admit that Freddie's words hit home. More importantly than the other man's physical appearance, however, was Tanner's knowledge that, of all the people he knew and worked alongside, Freddie was the only one who didn't feel jealous or envious over the level of power that Tanner commanded. For that simple reason - he didn't fear being backstabbed - Tanner trusted Freddie enough to share all sorts of intimate details of his life.

"Eh, you get used to it." Freddie shrugged. "Now, what sort of fun did you have last night, while the rest of us were in bed like normal people?"

"It eventually ended up in a bed," Tanner said slyly, and Freddie punched him lightly in the shoulder while rolling his eyes. "But I just went to Billy Martin's and tracked down Senator Waltz. Send a few ladies his way, plied them with some champagne, and snuck a few photographs. Easy job."

Freddie shook his head in admiration. "You say that so casually, but you're playing with people's careers! One of these days, you know that you're going to get burned by this."

"Not me," Tanner disagreed. "And when I confronted Waltz this morning, he gave in right away. Look, Freddie, this is just the way that politics really works in this town. It's all about leverage."

"The realist in me knows that what you're saying is true, but the optimist inside me, battered and beaten, keeps hoping that you'll get your comeuppance at some point." Freddie swallowed the last of his beer, dropping the pint glass down heavily onto the wooden bar rail. "You know, that bartender's sure taking a while with your drink. Maybe your flirting game isn't as good as you think."

"Worked on the girls last night," Tanner replied. "When it turned out that Waltz didn't quite have the… energy to perform, shall we say, they were happy to accept me as a substitute." He grinned. "And while the brunettes put in a good effort, the blonde stole the show. She could fit both her legs back behind her head, and still use her arms to-"

He stopped, seeing that Freddie had raised his fingers and plugged both his ears. "Enough, stop torturing me!" he burst out, wincing good-naturedly. "Come on, I know that you're a god at pulling in slutty women, but you drive me crazy with these stories!"

"Then why do you keep wanting to hear them?"

He shrugged. "Torturing myself, maybe? Or maybe I'm just eagerly awaiting the day when the great, all-powerful Keegan Tanner finally meets his match and gets taken down a peg, knocked back down to the level of the rest of us mortals."

"May that day never come," Tanner added, lifting his empty hand as if holding a wineglass for a toast.

"Your drink, sir - sorry that it took so long."

Both of the men glanced up as the bartender reappeared, placing a glass of scotch in front of Tanner. "Again, I'm sorry that there was a wait," she repeated, leaning forward with her elbows on the bar and giving the two men a clear look at her expanse of creamy white cleavage on display. "But I'm done with my shift, now, and I feel awful, just awful. Please, let me know if there's anything at all that I can do to make you feel better." Her lazy wink at Tanner left no ambiguity as to the hidden meaning behind these words.

Next to him, Freddie groaned as he leaned away from the bar. "God, man, it's like the gods blessed you with some sort of pheromones or something, and I just have to sit by and watch."

Tanner smiled back at the bartender, leaning forward so that their faces were less than a foot apart. "That's very generous of you..."

"Courtney," she filled in, blinking her long lashes back at him.

"Courtney," he repeated. "And what do I owe you for the drink?"

"Let's call it on the house - but you can find a way to repay me for it," she purred, squeezing her eyes into slits for a moment. Her gaze flicked over to Freddie, losing a bit of its seductiveness. "Your total is fourteen dollars, by the way."

Freddie grumbled and reached for his wallet, but Tanner laid a hand on his friend's arm. "Let me cover his bill," he said to Courtney, standing up. "After all, what are friends for?"

"What a nice man!" Courtney said, her eyes never leaving Tanner, watching with a satisfied smile as his own gaze drifted down to her expansive chest before returning back up. "So thoughtful and generous."

Tanner smiled back at her, his eyes not moving from her face even as he took a sip of his scotch. Perfect. "Very generous," he agreed, already thinking of how he'd undress her, claim her soft body with his own hard one, make her scream out his name as he used her ruthlessly for his own pleasure.

CHAPTER THREE

"Ah, Tanner! Good of you to make it, sorry for the wait. Come on in."

Tanner rose up from the black leather couch, tossing aside the tattered copy of The Economist that he'd been idly leafing through. He hadn't been waiting long - the receptionist at the desk had not yet returned with the coffee he requested, although he readily admitted that this delay was, at least in part, his own fault. He'd been flirting with her hard enough to make her stammer and blush, and she insisted on jotting down her phone number for him before darting off to fetch his beverage.

Still, it wasn't as if he'd turn away a summons from Richard Pribus, head of the Republican National Committee and the closest thing that Tanner had to a direct boss. Pribus had managed the RNC for years, now, and although he put on a kind and patrician face for the public, the man acted like a ruthless killer behind the scenes. He showed no hesitation in resorting to underhanded methods to pursue the RNC's goals when more overt and bipartisan measures failed.

And when he decided to go in a sneakier direction, Tanner was usually the first one to get a call.

Tanner buttoned his suit as he stood up from where he'd been waiting. Out of the corner of his eye, he spotted the receptionist finally returning with his coffee, and he relieved her of the steaming cup with a peck on the cheek. She blushed as she settled back down behind her desk, and Tanner breezed into Pribus's office as he lifted the cup to his lips.

In his expansive office, Pribus was already settling in behind his massive wooden desk, sighing a little. "You know, I'd prefer if you didn't flirt with the help," he complained as Tanner took the seat in front of the desk. "We go through enough accusations of sexual harassment as it is."

"Hey, I stop whenever they ask," Tanner pointed out.

"Yeah, but with you, they don't ask you to stop," Pribus countered.

Tanner smirked at him. "I don't see the problem."

"The problem," his boss elaborated, "happens when they all start talking to each other, and they realize that they've all gotten the same treatment from you."

"Hey, I never told them that we were exclusive!" Tanner kept up his smirk, knowing that Pribus wouldn't stay on this issue forever. Not when he clearly had an actual assignment for Tanner to undertake.

Sure enough, after another sigh, Pribus dropped the issue. "At least don't do it so blatantly, okay?" he groaned. "But that's not what I called you in here for today."

"Is this about any issues with the Waltz thing?" Looking over the crowded stacks of paper and other items that littered the top of Pribus's massive desk, Tanner spotted the envelope that he'd handed off to Charlie the night before. Looks like the old security guard came through for him again, he thought happily. No issues there - not that the pictures even proved necessary, given how quickly Waltz had caved and capitulated.

"No, no, that went fine." Pribus flicked his eyes briefly towards the envelope, then back up to Tanner. "Nice job with that, by the way. You always make these jobs seem so easy."

Outwardly, Tanner just grinned, pretending that the compliment didn't warm him on the inside. Inside his head, however, he couldn't help preening, just a little bit. Not even halfway through his career, and already considered as the top fixer for the RNC!

"And that," Pribus continued, "is why I think that you'll be perfect for this next little issue that we're tackling." He reached for a manilla folder, but paused, looking back at Tanner. "It's a particularly tricky one, but we think that you've got the right skills to handle it."

Tanner just held out his hand. After a moment longer, gazing across the massive expanse of burnished wood at him, Pribus handed over the folder.

With a flip, Tanner opened up the folder on his lap. The name and picture of his target greeted him on the very first page, staring up at him with intense focus.

"Alicia Stone?" he read off, frowning slightly.

"That's right," Pribus confirmed. "She's the freshman senator from Colorado. Just arrived here, but she's already aiming to shake things up in a major way - one that doesn't exactly flow with our goals."

That was a hell of an understatement, Tanner knew. He'd watched as Stone, a young upstart with no prior political experience, managed to somehow sweep the election in Colorado, winning her Senate seat in a landslide victory. Of course, Colorado had always been a largely blue state, so Stone's victory wasn't impossible to imagine - but she cleared away the incumbent, Gary Gardener, with a strong message of empowerment and change. Despite her youth and inexperience, she was already attracting attention on the national stage.

Of course she'd pose a concern for Pribus and the Republicans, Tanner knew. Not only was Stone a largely unknown factor, without much of a voting record to be used strategically against her, but she also seemed to have a natural gift for public speaking. Her strong, passionate, firebrand style never failed to energize a crowd - and that energy seemed to persist long after she left the podium. She'd spoken out strongly in favor of gun control, and several Republican congressmen reported receiving record numbers of calls to their offices over the following week.

"Tell me more," Tanner said to Pribus. He knew that there was more information in the packet on his lap, but he didn't want to sit and read it. He'd pore over every detail in the folder later on, but not now, not here.

"Well, our biggest concern is her newest project, the one that got her elected. This American Quality Education bill - you've heard of it?"

Of course Tanner had heard of it. The American Quality Education Bill had been one of the biggest planks in Alicia Stone's platform when she ran for Senate. She pointed an accusing finger at the education system in general, and Republicans in particular, as the source of many of the country's ills. She promised to divert many more millions of dollars to education spending over the next few years, and swore to make this her number one priority during her time as senator, even going so far as to say that, if she failed at this goal, she wouldn't bother attempting to seek re-election when her term was up.

Pribus gave Tanner a brief recap of the bill, just in case he'd somehow had his head under a rock for the last election cycle. "This thing is going to look very bad for us," he finished, shaking his head back and forth. "I mean, wasteful spending, on public education no less, is totally against our principles - but if we take a stand against this, we're going to be absolutely battered by this thing, over and over, you know?"

"Sure," Tanner agreed. "You support this, and our supporters will accuse us of wasteful spending. We stand against it, and we'll get blamed for mortgaging the future of our children."

Pribus pointed across his desk at Tanner. "Nailed it, right on the nose. This thing gets us either way. And that's where you come in."

"Me?"

"Yep. Your newest job is to kill this thing. I don't know how, don't know what it will take to get rid of it, but I want it gone. And I suspect that the easiest way to kill it is to cut off the head." He pointed over his desk at the folder sitting in Tanner's lap. "That means getting to this freshman and showing her that, just because she charged up the yokels back in Colorado, it doesn't mean that she'll be able to have her way here in Washington. Understand?"

Tanner looked back down at the still-open folder in his lap. This time, instead of reading through any of the enclosed documents, most of which contained information on the bill and what it might contain, he focused his attention on the picture of Alicia Stone.

Pretty, he thought to himself. That, just by itself, was a rarity among the Washington elite. Oh, sure, most of the men did their best to look esteemed and handsome, but the women who ran in high powered circles didn't go for pretty. Pretty suggested vulnerable, suggested weakness, suggested that they could be exploited.

No, most of the women who held office, or held positions of power behind an office, dressed for authority. They usually wore smart pantsuits that hid their curves, loose outfits to try and make them look more like their male counterparts. They generally eschewed makeup, wearing the wrinkles on their faces as badges of honor, cutting their hair short or pushing it away in no-nonsense haircuts. In short, they did everything possible to hide the fact that they were female.

But not Alicia, Tanner thought to himself as he studied her picture. Either she didn't yet understand the Washington power culture enough to change her look, or she didn't care.

Instead of pulling her hair back in a bun, or cutting it short in a bob, she let it spill out and cascade down the sides of her head, falling in waves over her shoulders. The photograph was taken only from the shoulders up, but her suit looked well fitted, tighter than the baggy outfits that most female politicians chose. Her face reflected her youth - Tanner knew that she was only in her late twenties - but gleamed with determination, confidence, charisma.

If he saw her in a bar, even not knowing who she was, he'd be more than willing to give her a smile.

And that would be his way in.

Glancing up from the photograph, Tanner saw Pribus still looking at him, waiting for a response. "Well?" the head of the Republican National Committee asked again, looking a little more worried and haggard than he usually appeared in public. "Are you going to be able to make this problem go away for us?"

Tanner held his tongue for just a moment longer, saving the other man's need for his help. Without him, Pribus would be caught on the horns of this dilemma, stuck searching for another way out. The old man needed Tanner's skills, knew that Tanner was likely the only fixer on the Republican payroll who'd be willing to even try to accomplish this. The man was proposing something immoral, if not outright illegal, and he knew that Tanner knew all of this as well.

"This shouldn't be a problem," Tanner said, and he bit back his smile as Pribus let out an audible sigh of relief, his shoulders relaxing and slumping back down.

"Great, great," Pribus said, trying to act as if he'd known all along that Tanner would agree. "And of course, whatever you need - you've got the usual slush fund to pay for any expenses, and we'll be sure to pay you handsomely once the bill is dead. We can set you up with whatever documents you might need, and of course if you need any more support from Republicans, maybe for some sort of quid pro quo deal, just let me know and I'm sure that we can discuss amenable terms…"

Tanner tuned out as Pribus babbled on. His eyes dropped back down to the picture sitting in the folder on his lap as he thought about his next steps.

Treat this like a chess game. The goal wasn't just to charge in and be the first to a spot. That was a sure way to get cut off, to be outflanked and surrounded, brought down like ancient hunters teaming up against a mammoth. No, he needed to instead be strategic, plot out all of his moves several steps ahead. By the time he made the first move, he'd already know the entire path to victory.

But given Alicia Stone's inexperience with Washington, with the rules of power here, Tanner didn't foresee much of a struggle. She would take him at face value, never expect for someone to double-cross her. He would slip in, earn her confidence - and then, just when she gave him the keys to everything, he'd snatch it all away.

He stood up, setting down his half-finished coffee on the corner of Pribus's desk. "I had better get started," he announced, and left the RNC leader's office.

The receptionist outside of Pribus's office gave Tanner a flirty wave, but he didn't even notice. All of his attention was on Alicia, thinking about the game that lay ahead.

Time to make the first move.

CHAPTER FOUR

Several hours later, Tanner rubbed at his eyes as he leaned back, away from the slim laptop sitting open on the coffee table in front of him. His eyes flicked over the remains of a ham and cheese sandwich, but he instead reached for the cup of coffee, tossing back the last gulp in the cup. He briefly considered another refill, but he'd already drank three cups while sitting here, and he could feel his eyeballs practically beginning to vibrate.

He'd put in the research, utterly focused on one person: Alicia Stone.

She was quite the impressive woman, Tanner had to admit. He'd read everything on her that he could find, doing his best to gather a complete picture of her. He needed to make sure that the persona he projected when meeting her would be calculated for maximum impact on her.

Alicia Stone, it seemed, had always been a high achiever. Second in her class in high school. "Nearly valedictorian," she'd said ruefully in an interview. "That was probably the first time when I failed at something, and it really taught me that all the hard things take real work. Until then, I'd breezed by. But after losing out for that top spot, I declared that I wouldn't coast my way through anything else."

Apparently, that high standard also applied to the men that she dated - or that she didn't date, more accurately. Tanner switched over to another tab on his browser, this one displaying the video from an interview with her when she'd been running for the Senate seat. "Nope, no significant other in the picture right now," she told the interviewer, smiling at the camera and flashing a dimple. "Focused on my career right now, and helping the good people of Colorado. I think that, before I start thinking about getting into a relationship and whatever might come after that, I need to work to make sure that this world is good enough for whatever the future might hold."

Carter paused the video there, taking a moment to make a little gagging face at his computer screen. That little quip just screamed soundbyte, and Alicia and her team of speechwriters had probably reworked it a dozen times before settling on the final phrasing. It made it clear that she wasn't going to be distracted with romance as she did her job, but also gave a little hint to the possible future of a husband and children; the good American wife doing some public service to better her country before returning home to care for her two and a half children in the perfect little apple-cheeked family.

Still, even if speechwriters had polished the final quote, it came from Alicia's lips. She was a high achiever, career focused woman for the moment, but possibly looking for more in the future, not the kind of woman who wanted to just mess around and have a bit of short-sighted fun. She strove for the best, and wouldn't settle for anything less.

A little bit of Tanner's spirit flared up, perhaps sensing a kindred soul. Not that they truly had much in common, but he respected Alicia's refusal to compromise. Tanner compromised all the time - he knew that this was how the real world worked, after all - but each time he settled for something that he knew was less than perfect, a little part of his mind winced.

Fortunately for Tanner, Alicia still faced the problem that nearly every freshman arrival to Congress encountered. Sure, running a campaign was a big challenge, but it didn't usually translate well to acting as a sitting Senator or Representative.

In short, Alicia needed help getting organized for tackling the challenges of Washington.

And that, he decided, would be his opening.

Tanner closed his computer, pulling out his phone instead. He opened up his contacts, scrolling through the long list, searching for the perfect name. He needed someone to make the introduction, someone trustworthy but not totally rock solid. Just enough for him to get the interview - and then, face to face, he could seal the deal. Throw in just a tiny bit of flirting, enough to keep her off balance ever so slightly, and she'd be open to his ideas. He knew exactly how to run a staff here, and he'd easily land the job, giving him full access to Alicia.

And then, from there, he'd just need a little more work to build up her trust, and she'd soon be willing to spill everything.

Pausing for a moment as he scrolled through a seemingly never-ending list of names, Tanner stopped, trying to decide how he'd play the endgame. He could send Alicia home with her tail between her legs, of course; that would be as easy as pulling the same "pictures leaked on the internet" scam that had worked so well with Senator Waltz. Women were even more susceptible to that approach than men, he'd found. Even though both men and women were equally at blame, the social stigma always seemed to predominantly target the woman. A honeypot trap would ruin her.

But maybe he didn't need to fully destroy Alicia. He could perhaps steer her in another direction, crush the bill but keep the senator alive. After all, she'd be another screw that he could turn, another little toy that Tanner could use when he needed a favor, needed to help make something else happen. He had several senators already in his pocket, but there was always room for one more.

In any case, Tanner didn't need to decide on the end game just yet. He'd get in, earn Alicia's confidences, and then make the decision as to what would work best.

Almost a pity to destroy her, he mused, glancing back down at the picture of her that he'd removed from the manilla folder. He'd drawn it out so he could study it, memorize every little line and feature and detail of her face.

It really was quite a pretty face. Not the kind of face that belonged in a Spring Break video above a pair of happily bobbing tits, mind you, but the kind of face that he wouldn't mind seeing at brunch. The kind of girl that he'd happily bring home to his parents.

For a moment, that stray thought made Tanner hesitate, his conscience unexpectedly flaring up. A crack of sorrow shone through at the mental mention of his parents, like a sapling determined to break through a concrete sidewalk barrier.

Viciously, he fought it back down. He'd come this far, earned this much power and respect and command. He wasn't about to throw it all away, to back down now. He'd made his sacrifices.

Still a bit annoyed with himself, he took another bite of his sandwich, brushing away the crumbs that fell on his dress shirt and tie. He'd hung his jacket over the back of his chair, but a few crumbs still clung to the shining white linen fabric of his shirt. He carefully flicked every last one away.

Back to the task at hand. He found the number he'd

been seeking in his phone, held it up to his ear as it rang.

"Hello Aaron," he said, as soon as the call connected. "Got a minute? I need a favor from you."

Patiently, Tanner exchanged a bit of small talk with Aaron Perkins, chief of staff for Senator Harrison Reed. Reed was one of the longest-serving Democrats in the Senate, but he tended to stay under the radar most of the time, not rising up to address many of the hot-button issues of the current media cycle. Reed also gave off an almost paternal air to everyone he met, like a gentle father swallowing his vague disappointment in his children. He'd be the perfect source of an introduction to Alicia and her disorganized campaign.

"Well, that's actually part of why I'm calling," he jumped in as soon as he sensed an opening in the conversation. "Aaron, I'm looking to take a step away from my current duties. And I had my eye on Alicia Stone, the new senator out of Colorado."

He paused for a moment as Aaron made a rather off-color comment, forcing himself to chuckle politely. "Yes, that one. The looker. I mean, I won't say that it's not at least a small part of how I made the decision!" He waited again as Aaron laughed again.

"But here's my problem, Aaron," he went on after the laughter subsided. "I've got a lot of connections on the Republican side - which could certainly prove useful to Alicia, you can't deny - but not so many on the Democrat side. I know that Alicia's got a big bill on her mind, and I want to offer my help."

Another pause, and this time Tanner frowned as he listened to Aaron's incredulous comments.

"I do so have a heart!" he retorted. "And listen, this is my chance to prove it to you. I've been thinking about…" he searched his mind for the best word to use. "Legacy, Aaron. Don't you think about the legacy that you'll leave behind?"

Tanner grinned to himself at the response from Aaron. That had definitely been the right word to choose. All Democrats, even their most hardened campaign staffers, ate up this bullshit like it was candy. Too focused on plastering their name on something in the future, not thinking enough about getting power today. Their perennial weakness.

"Exactly, I'm glad that you get it," he cut in after he'd let Aaron go on for a bit. "And Alicia's bill could be my chance to do something big. I've got quite a lot of favors built up, on both sides. And just because the RNC has been calling me in a lot as of late, that doesn't mean that they own my allegiance. I just want to help move things forward, make sure that everyone gets what they want." Inside his head, he made a little gagging noise at this softness. How could anyone really believe in this shit?

But Aaron evidently did. Just as Tanner had anticipated, the man's tone softened, turning affirmative. "Great," Tanner slipped in, not wanting to spend all afternoon on the phone as the chief of staff recounted all the little inconsequential things he'd done to try and secure his own legacy. "So could you get me a meeting with Senator Stone?"

He sighed. "No, not with her staff. Come on, Aaron, don't bullshit me like that. We both know that she's brand new here. She's got nothing for staff, at least nothing permanent. She's barely even set up shop here. She's still going to be scrambling. Hell, that's half the reason that I picked her."

Finally, Aaron came around. "Great. Tomorrow morning, yes, my schedule's fairly open. Just send me the details, and I'll squeeze it in." Tanner rolled his eyes again at Aaron's next off-color crack, but didn't let his annoyance show in his tone. "Hey, I'm only squeezing it in there if she gives me permission! You know how picky they get about making sure it's all consensual!"

Tanner moved the phone slightly further from his ear as Aaron guffawed. Yes, the boys' club attitude in Washington was still alive and well. Women might have made significant progress in breaking through the glass ceiling in the corporate world, but they were still barely beginning to chip away at the thick layer of sexism in DC.

He rushed through the rest of his small talk with Aaron and got off the phone at the first available opportunity. Sighing, he set the phone down, shaking his head. He forgot, sometimes, how tiresome it could be to deal with all these little toadies, each one puffed up with his own self-importance and needing to be massaged and coerced into seeing things from Tanner's point of view.

He glanced down at his watch. He'd meet with Alicia tomorrow morning, but he had the rest of the evening open. He'd need his sleep, would need to be up bright and early to get ready for this meeting. No clubbing for him tonight.

He did, however, still have the number of that blonde bartender from the Capitol Lounge. What was her name - Candy? She'd given him quite the enjoyable evening the night before, ending with a wonderfully wet and enthusiastic blowjob, right on the front steps outside her apartment building!

Tanner grinned. Just thinking about her big, heavy tits and that soft, wet mouth was giving him a chub! He could head home, hit the gym and pump some iron for an hour or so, and then grab a quick shower and let Candy into his own luxurious apartment. A bottle of wine, maybe cook her some dinner - girls ate that shit up. He'd have her naked and on all fours, moaning as he took her, before midnight.

Briefly, as he tucked away his computer and headed out of the cafe, he wondered whether Alicia was wild in bed. He likely wouldn't get that far with her, but he still allowed himself a moment of fantasy. Maybe all that repressed good girl attitude was hiding an absolute wildcat in the sack.

Wouldn't that be just his luck?

CHAPTER FIVE

A single glance around Alicia's new Washington, DC office the next morning revealed that Tanner's guess was right on the mark. The walls were still covered with unframed posters from her election campaign, many of them tacked up at haphazard angles as if put up by drunken staffers celebrating her recent win. Those staffers were probably all unaware, of course, that the relocation to Washington would end up putting most of them out of a job.

"A nice place," he said politely to the bespectacled little man in front of him, leading him through the office.

The man - George Duecent, he'd named himself - just shook his head, using one finger to push his glasses up as they started to slip down his nose. "We've worked out of worse," he muttered, not slowing as his little legs flew back and forth to move him along in a scurrying sort of motion.

Tanner turned sideways to slip through the narrow gap between two desks as he followed after Duecent. He'd spent almost an hour getting ready this morning, spending time considering every single choice in his outfit. He'd ended up going with his cheapest, most wrinkled suit, pairing it with an older white shirt that bore a couple faint hints of bleached-out coffee stains. Of course, Tanner had carefully sponged the coffee onto those locations before washing it away, but nobody else knew that, and the shirt and suit combination gave the impression of someone who considered his appearance, but didn't make it his highest priority. The knot on his blue tie was ever so slightly off-center, adding to the illusion.

Looking around, Tanner wondered if, even with these steps down from his typical wardrobe, he might still have come slightly overdressed. He didn't see another sportcoat in the entire office - Duecent wore slacks and a baggy white shirt with an obvious marinara stain on the collar - and several of the staffers were even dressed in jeans, for chrissake! Bunch of yokels, the lot of them.

A moment later, however, Tanner reminded himself that he shouldn't be thinking in such a fashion. He needed to sell himself as, if not one of these hayseeds, at least someone who could work with them, get along with them. So as he followed after Duecent, he peeled off his jacket and slung it over his shoulder to better reveal the coffee-stained shirt.

"And here we are," Duecent said, stopping at a door. "Senator Stone's office." He glared up at Tanner, a full foot shorter but scowling ferociously. Tanner had to shake off the illusion that a bulldog had managed to crawl into some formal clothes and now stood before him.

"Great, thank you," Tanner said. Duecent was one of those types who prided himself on his prickly, asshole attitude, he guessed. So instead of a smile or a handshake, he just gave a short little nod, flashing his teeth in more of a grimace than a smile. He wanted to convey the impression that offering up thanks was physically painful.

Duecent didn't smile, but his glare lessened slightly, which Tanner took as a good sign. "Head on in - she'll call me if she needs anything," he said, and turned away.

No offer of coffee, no warnings about Alicia's current mood, no introduction on his behalf. Duecent might prove to be a tough nut to crack. Tanner made a mental note to ask around about what the chief of staff might like, so he could bring him a present to crack the ice.

For the moment, however, he needed to focus instead on Alicia. Charming Alicia was most important; everything else was secondary. He took a deep breath, let it out slowly as he shook out his shoulders. He could still feel a comforting little residual burn in his muscles; the sign of a good workout the day before.

And then he turned the knob and stepped into Senator Alicia Stone's office.

Not bad, was his first thought as his eyes quickly took in the interior of the little room. And that went for the woman behind the desk, as well as the decorations.

Alicia's office was small, of course; junior Senators always received the worst accommodations. Unlike the outside rooms, however, Alicia had either brought in a designer, or taken the time and effort to make her new office feel a bit more comfortable. Dark cherry bookshelves lined one entire wall; running his eyes over the titles, Tanner observed that, along with books of law and history, Alicia also had some newer thrillers, biographies, and even a couple of romance titles among the older and dustier hardcovers! She'd rolled out a thick rug over the floor, and an oil painting of the Rocky Mountains, done in an Impressionist style, hung behind her chair. Some senators chose to cover their office walls in photographs of themselves, smiling and shaking hands with various important or famous people, but Tanner only saw a few small pictures on Alicia's walls - and he didn't recognize the faces of the men and women standing next to Alicia, smiling and shaking her hand.

After the quick sweep around the office, Tanner

focused his eyes on the woman now rising up from behind her desk. "Hello there, Senator Stone," he said, putting on his carefully chosen smile (confident but not too haughty, interested and open, self-assured but not yet straying into arrogance). "It's good to meet you."

"And you too, Mr. Tanner," Alicia returned, accepting his handshake across the desk. She had a good grip, despite the delicate fingers, Tanner noted. It wasn't the politician's overly hearty handshake, however; it suggested interest, but also a slight detachment. "Mr. Perkins spoke highly of you."

"Thank you for taking the time to meet with me," Tanner replied, brushing off the compliment. "Indeed, I've been watching your campaign with some interest. You've done quite the exemplary job, so far."

"Oh?" Alicia asked, leaning forward a little as Tanner took a seat across from her desk. He crossed his legs but leaned forward; interested but not threatening.

"Yes, you've done an amazing job," he went on, doing his best to walk the line between too much praise and too little. "And I've also been quite interested in your platform - very audacious!" He chuckled, showing that he didn't mean this as a slight. "But although you've definitely got the fire, I suspect that you might be in need of someone with a bit more experience in navigating the Washington waters. Someone who can help clear the way to make accomplishing your big goals a little easier."

"And that someone is you, I'm guessing," Alicia commented, giving him a little smile.

He smiled back - easy, engaging, charming. "Well, I do have some experience in this area," he said, casting his eyes downward, not wanting to make his brag seem too obvious. "I've been around long enough to make plenty of connections, on both sides of the aisle. I think that, between your ambition and my experience, we could weave a very strong legacy."

There. Magic word deployed. Sure enough, he saw Alicia's eyes - blue-green eyes, quite enchanting - flash at the mention of a legacy. Democrats must have some genetic weakness to that word, he considered to himself.

"And what position do you see yourself in, exactly?" Alicia asked, pushing her chair back. She rose up and moved around from behind the desk, taking a seat on the chair next to Tanner.

Tanner found himself needing to focus quite hard to keep his eyes from darting to her legs. Alicia wore the typical blouse and pencil skirt, professional and uptight, but it was cut a little closer to her figure than the Washington standard, revealing a very nice pair of legs. He kept his eyes carefully up on her face, not giving away the slightest hint of his inner surge of lust. "Well, perhaps a senior advisor role," he replied easily. "I wouldn't want to presume to tell you how to structure your staff, but the closer we work together, the easier it will be for me to open doors for you."

"Working closely does sound like a good idea," Alicia murmured, leaning forward slightly towards him.

Not showing any sign of inner turmoil, Tanner hastily recalculated. She was coming onto him! Very subtle, but he could see her pupils dilating slightly, the way that she noted his broad shoulders, even disguised beneath the somewhat baggy and ill-fitting suit. Barely arrived in Washington and already searching for a sexual partner - perhaps Alicia Stone was adapting to the Washington culture faster than he'd anticipated!

Still, this was good news. He could use this - and indeed, it just advanced the timetable of his overall plan. This was just what he'd been hoping to see. The goal now would be to flirt back without being the first one to make a move. Alicia, despite her youth, seemed to want to lead.

"And where might it be best to focus first?" Alicia asked, those big blue-green eyes still locked on him. "In your personal opinion?"

Those eyes were surprisingly deep and distracting. To Tanner's own surprise, he had to focus quite hard to keep from getting lost in them. "Well, on your campaign for this seat, you discussed your education bill quite regularly," he said. "That might be a good place to start - although we'll want to move slowly at first, not rush ahead too quickly."

"What's wrong with rushing ahead? Sometimes it's best to just dive in," Alicia countered, a little smile darting about her lips. Tanner swallowed at the heat in her voice. She really wasn't holding back!

"Well, it's a very complex process, especially if you don't want it to go down in flames," he managed. "Need to get everyone on board. We don't want to be accused of anything… improper."

He lingered on that last word, seeing another little flare of Alicia's pupils. Yes, she definitely wanted him! He couldn't believe that things were going to be this easy. Then again, this was where he excelled. He, Keegan Tanner, was a master in the arena of seduction, and this poor young woman, new to the kind of deep politics played in Washington, didn't stand a chance against him.

He almost felt sorry for her.

"Improper," Alicia repeated, her voice deeper, huskier. God, that was a sexy voice. Tanner couldn't quite help himself any longer - his eyes dipped down briefly, noting that, as she leaned forward, her blouse gaped open slightly at the neckline. It wasn't enough to be improper, but he caught the slightest little glimpse of her breasts, soft and supple. Heat flared deep inside of him, surging down his spine and stiffening his cock inside his pants. "Is that truly what you want to avoid, Mr. Tanner?"

"Well, we don't want anything to get out in public," Tanner murmured back, mesmerized by this seductress, eagerly opening herself up to him. This was too easy!

"But in private…"

"Well, we do need to indulge in fantasies every now

and then," he allowed. "After all, we all do fantasize about what we want to accomplish..." His words, technically, could still be proper, still be about the legal process - but heat flared in Alicia's eyes, and he knew that an answering flame was burning in his own.

She didn't say anything else, but leaned in a little closer. This was it! Tanner matched her, one of his hands rising up. Once their lips met, he'd cup her neck, draw her to him. Of course, he wouldn't fully take her, not here - but she'd hire him on, they could arrange a suitable off-site location to meet that evening, and he'd just arrive early to set up the cameras so that he could gather the blackmail material he needed...

So close to him, Alicia's lips parted. "I know what you want, Mr. Tanner," she whispered, and Tanner felt himself grow even harder, throbbing inside his pants.

"What is that?" he asked back, his gaze locked on hers, looking into those soft, limpid pools of greenish blue, filled with heat and desire and warmth-

-and then, like a door slamming shut, all the heat vanished from her eyes.

"I know, Mr. Tanner," Alicia repeated. She still whispered, but this time there was a new hardness to her voice, a lining of steel, sharp as a blade. "I know exactly what you want - and who you are."

Confusion shot through Tanner's head. This wasn't what she was supposed to say.

He started to draw back, but Alicia's hand shot out. She closed her fist on his tie, keeping him close. With a yank, the knot tightened uncomfortably on his neck.

"Oh, Mr. Tanner," Alicia said again, her voice no longer that seductive whisper, now hard as diamonds, edged with ice. "I asked about, found out all about you. What you do. Did you really think that I'd be so easy?"

Tanner opened his mouth, but for once in his life, he found himself speechless.

Somewhere, along the way, he'd made a horrible miscalculation.

And now, as Alicia glared at him, chilling him to the bone, he had a horrible feeling that, for the first time in his memory, he'd gotten himself in over his head…

CHAPTER SIX

Alicia glared at the scumbag sitting in her office. His face no longer showed the brief flash of confusion - that had been quickly swept away; the man had excellent poker skills, at least - but he was definitely off balance.

Good. Served him right, for what he just attempted to do.

Duecent, Alicia's campaign manager when she ran for office, now serving as her interim chief of staff, had simply told Alicia that she had a meeting with Keegan Tanner the next morning.

"And who is this Mr. Tanner?" Alicia asked, frowning at the little bulldog of a man as he hesitated in the entrance to her office, wavering as if not sure whether he should invite himself in or duck and bow like a proper servant.

In response, Duecent just shrugged. "Comes recommended by Aaron Perkins, from Senator Reed's office," he answered. "I guess he's got a lot of connections around here, senior fellow, and he wants to try and help you out. Given that you're new here, and all."

"Well, that's very kind of Mr. Tanner," Alicia

murmured, her bullshit detector buzzing at high alert. "Did you find out anything else about him?"

All she got back was another shrug. Duecent had been a great campaign manager, Alicia considered as she watched the man finally decide to leave the threshold of her office and head off to do… something, but he wasn't exactly cut out to be a great Chief of Staff for her office. Perhaps this Tanner fellow could help out on that front.

But instead of leaving the matter there, Alicia grabbed her computer and typed Keegan Tanner's name into the search bar on Google. She clicked over to the images tab for a moment, looking at the top pictures that came up.

The top dozen hits were all for the same man, and Alicia decided that this must be Mr. Tanner. He was quite attractive, she thought, and younger than she'd expected. Something about his expression, however - the smile that spoke of hours practicing in front of the mirror, the perfectly groomed hair, the broad shoulders that had been built in a gym, not out in a field - gave her the impression of a shark. Keegan Tanner looked ready to take a bite out of any juicy target that he could find.

Next, Alicia moved over to the list of returned results, and began reading. She moved quickly and methodically through the list of links, ferreting out all the information that she could uncover.

Research. Alicia had always prided herself on it. It sounded like a cold and solitary pursuit, she admitted readily enough, but ever since she was a little girl, she'd loved packing her head full of facts, arming herself with weapons of knowledge, wrapping herself in the armor of education. Her dad used to joke that, when he came home from work, he was more likely to find Alicia in the family's little library, curled up around a book, than in her room playing with her toys.

Despite his jokes, however, both Alicia's mother and father encouraged her to learn. Instead of insisting that she should be playing dress-up with her Barbies and throwing tea parties with the stuffed animals that well-meaning relatives kept on sending her for birthday presents, they put up with her twice-a-month visits to the local public library. Most of the time, Alicia staggered out of the library with both hands wrapped around a stack of books that reached nearly all the way up to her chin. The librarians chuckled - up until she came back two weeks later, returning them all and exchanging them for a fresh stack.

The lessons of research stuck with Alicia, and she always made an effort to know as much as possible about any meeting or debate that she entered. When it came time for her weekly call home to her parents, updating them on their girl's progress in the big world of politics, she often had to drag herself away from an open book to pick up the phone. Occasionally, she'd lose track of time as she stayed up late, reading up on points for a debate, only to glance up at the clock and realize that it was nearly three in the morning.

Fortunately, she didn't have a significant other to annoy with her odd hours - or, at least, that's what she told herself. A couple of times, she'd considered adopting a cat or a dog, some sort of companion to keep her company on those late nights, but the pollsters told her that she'd look less appealing if she chose a pet. "Speaks of desperation," they'd said.

Alicia didn't like hearing that the desire to own an animal companion made her desperate, but she did want to win. So she held off on adopting a cat or dog, and ended up sweeping the election by a landslide.

Reading through the links that Google returned on Keegan Tanner, Alicia found her nose prickling - the sure sign of bullshit being slathered on thickly. The man didn't seem to have any official title, but he popped up at plenty of political events and in the news, often quoted as simply "a Washington insider." For someone who didn't appear to have a formal job title, however, he certainly seemed to have a lot of inside connections.

That sounded dangerous to Alicia - why would he show any interest in a freshman Senator like herself? However, it also offered some possibility - if she could get him on her side, she desperately needed that expertise…

So when Keegan Tanner walked into her office a little later that morning, Alicia immediately sized him up, trying to guess his intentions.

He wore a slightly ill-fitting suit, with a couple of imperfectly cleaned coffee stains. That would suggest someone who wasn't too focused on their appearance - except that Alicia had seen the online pictures of Mr. Tanner, and knew that he loved his five thousand dollar suits. This, then, was all an act, a ruse to get close to her.

Well, two could play that game.

She turned up the charm, and to her surprise, she found the man falling for it! She did have to admit that he was quite attractive, objectively speaking, and she didn't need to try quite as hard to smile at him, batting her lashes, as she expected. Careful, Alicia, she warned herself. Don't get snared by him.

But then, Tanner eagerly charged forward, clearly doing his best to seduce her right here in this office, and Alicia reformed her defenses. She led him on, closer and closer to what he perceived as his target, getting a feel for him. Yes, he definitely had experience at this. She could tell from the buzzwords that he slipped carefully into the conversation that he knew how to play with people. If she hadn't known better, she might have even fallen for some of his lines.

As if Alicia would ever go for a man like this.

Running as a single woman… that had been a persistent thorn in her side, she had to admit. As much as she hated the idea of having to fight an uphill battle due to sexism (this was the twenty-first century! Sexism was supposed to be dead!), it turned out to be the reality of her campaign. She worked hard to establish herself as strong and independent, in order to court the female vote, while still making sure that she came off as attractive and fit, in order to appeal to the older, sexist men that formed an unfortunately large voting bloc.

A couple of times while on the campaign trail, Alicia even considered getting into a relationship, maybe even something serious, just so that she could drop this tired mantra of being a "strong and independent woman". There were a couple of cute reporters in the press corps that followed her around; maybe one of them would prove to be marriage material...

Alicia quickly squashed these thoughts whenever they emerged, and made sure that no trace of them slipped into her weekly talks with her parents. Privately, however, she did have to admit to herself that she was getting older, that she was getting tired of doing it all alone. Not that she'd give up her career for a husband; he'd have to be ready to handle her ambition and passion. But still, it would be nice to come home to someone, to curl up with another warm body on the couch and tell them all about her day, to have someone to complain to about the ridiculous comments made by fellow Senators and other Congressmen.

Tanner, however, despite his remarkably even and handsome features, that rugged set to his jaw, the strong body that couldn't be disguised by his ill-fitting suit, wasn't going to be that man.

He was, however, useful. Alicia just needed to apply the right pressure to guarantee that she saw results.

So she led him on - and then, just as he leaned forward, utterly confident that he had her eating out of the palm of his hand, she struck, both physically and verbally.

Her hand shot forward and grabbed his tie, dragging him down - that's right, Mr. Tanner, no using your height and male size to intimidate this lady! - and she stared into her eye. No more batting her eyes, no more sultry glances. She gave him her best icy, cold, emotionless stare, and she saw him swallow, his Adam's apple having a little trouble as his tie pulled tight around his neck.

Good.

Now, she just had to steer him in the right direction. All of that knowledge, all those connections in Tanner's head - those were the real value, here. Alicia knew that she needed that information. She couldn't do research on her fellow Senators, not in order to dig up the little nuggets of gossip and buried truth that would really do the most damage to them, would advance her cause the furthest. No, all those tempting little secrets were instead hidden in the heads of those "connected Washington insiders," men like Keegan Tanner.

But Tanner had to have visited her for a reason, something more than because he wanted to get his dick wet by taking advantage of a young and inexperienced new elected official. Alicia didn't know what his mission might be - maybe just fact-finding for the Republicans, maybe something more sinister - but right now, she'd have to keep that concern on the back burner.

She needed to maintain perfect control of the situation.

For the moment, Tanner was thrown off his mark, confused - but he would quickly recover. Alicia needed to keep him guessing, keep him off balance. If she never gave him the chance to figure out her plans, figure out her real goals, she could lead him to the path of least resistance.

So, still holding onto his tie, still perched on the chair beside him where she'd moved so that she could flirt more heavily, Alicia forced herself to relax. Shoulders back, don't hunch. Give him a little glimpse of the girls as you stretch your chest. Keep your legs crossed, letting that pencil skirt ride up just a tiny little bit, just enough to let him catch the quickest little glimpse of leg without seeming totally improper.

Watch as his eyes take the bait, darting to your chest, your legs, and then guiltily back up to your face.

Got you, Keegan Tanner. You're mine now.

All I need to do is reel you in.

Alicia's smile broadened, and this time she didn't need to make any effort for it to appear genuine. She muted it - no need to appear too eager - but inside her own head, she felt herself smiling like a cat, with a mouse trapped, helpless, in front of it.

She had Keegan Tanner right where she wanted him. She would convince him that he should take her side, would realize that she could see through all his bullshit. Of course, she suspected that this wouldn't be enough, on its own, to crush whatever was on his hidden agenda - but Alicia had faith that she'd be able to figure that out, too, and kill it before he could bring her down.

"Oh, Keegan," Alicia sighed, confident in having outmaneuvered her opponent. "Did you really think that it would be so easy to bring me down?"

CHAPTER SEVEN

Sitting in Senator Alicia Stone's office, Tanner felt the blood in his veins turn to ice as he realized, a little too late, that he'd made a horrible miscalculation.

He couldn't sit up, couldn't pull his head back, not with Alicia's grip on his tie threatening to strangle him. "What?" he managed weakly, thoughts still reeling.

Next to him, her legs still prettily crossed, Alicia shook her head. "Oh, Keegan," she said. "Did you really think that it would be so easy to bring me down? You thought that I was a rube, straight out of the sticks, someone that you could sweep off to bed with your big city charm and a few glasses of appropriately expensive wine? You could just steer me, young and malleable little me, in whatever direction your bosses wanted?"

"No, that's not…" Tanner trailed off, not even sure what to say. She'd outmaneuvered him, completely and horribly. He didn't even have a response, couldn't see a way to dig himself out of this trap.

He was screwed.

After giving it one last tug, Alicia finally released her

grip on his tie. Tanner quickly sat up, tugging the tie out of her reach as he slid one finger in between his neck and shirt to loosen it back up. Looking over at Alicia, he saw the same little smile playing about her lips that he'd spotted before.

This time, however, that smile wasn't sexy. That was the smile of a tiger, watching the final struggles of its helpless prey.

Alicia just sat there, watching him. Again, Tanner sensed that she was toying with him. He ran quickly through his options, but came up empty. He didn't have any other cards to play, no other smokescreens to hide behind. His shoulders slumped as the realization hit him.

"Fine." The word was soft, barely audible as it slipped out of his lips. "I'll get out of your office."

He started to stand - but again, fast as a striking cobra, Alicia's hand flew out and closed on his tie. Using it like a damn leash, she pulled him back down into the chair again.

"Hold on, no need to go rushing off," she replied, her smile widening. "After all, I still haven't told you if I'm hiring you or not."

Confused, Tanner sank back down into his chair once again. "What? But you just told me that you knew-" he began.

Alicia held up a finger. To his own amazement, Tanner felt his mouth snap shut halfway through his sentence. This woman seeing through his ruse had totally thrown him off balance. "I said that I know what you are, who sent you," she said. "But that doesn't mean that you're not still useful to me."

Tanner didn't open his mouth this time. He just sat, waiting. He felt a bit like a prisoner, looking up at the gallows and knowing that, sooner or later, it would be his turn to stand on that platform and feel the bite of rope around his neck.

"So," Alicia went on. "Here's my offer. You can

come to work for me - but you're on my side. You tell me when whatever Republicans that hold your strings give you orders, and you come up with excuses when I tell you to evade them." She glared at him, sending icy daggers into him. "And don't even think of lying to me. You try it, just once, and I'll burn you. Every single Democrat in this town will know that you're toxic, and I'll even do my best to make sure that every journalist puts you in their crosshairs. I'll make you crash and burn so hard that there won't be anything left of you except a little streak of carbon on the road. Got it?"

She stopped, waiting for Tanner to answer.

"Got it," he finally managed to choke out, still half-stunned.

He was screwed.

After another moment, Alicia's expression softened, ever so slightly. "Oh, don't look so dejected," she said. "It's really your own fault, of course, for underestimating me, but this won't be the worst thing you've done. You stick with me, and everyone else will think that you're helping to pass some great legislation, that you've turned around and decided to help the good guys for once. That phony 'legacy' speech you gave might turn out to be real, after all. What do you say?"

"Got it," he repeated again, as his mind still reeled. The good guys? She really was naive, if she thought that Washington could be simplified down to "good guys and bad guys". She'd need to open her eyes, and quickly, if she wanted to keep her skin around here.

But then again, he reminded himself, she'd seen through him. So maybe she wasn't as naive as he thought. That consideration sent a fresh sting of humiliation through him, but he suffered through it in silence.

Alicia stood up. "You might as well go ahead and gawk at me, now that I know your secrets," she commented idly. "After all, it's not like I don't work hard to make sure that I look good. Might as well show it off."

"I don't know what you're talking about," Tanner protested, even as his eyes shot to her body, greedily drinking in her lines and curves. She really wasn't kidding. That blouse and tight pencil skirt, although professional appearing at first glance, made it clear that an absolute knockout of a body lurked beneath the garments.

And the fact that she'd seen his lust for her, that she could tell even now how she excited him, made him even angrier with himself.

"So?" Alicia asked, as she sauntered back behind the desk and resumed her original seat. She leaned forward, locking eyes with him as she intertwined her fingers in front of her. "Do we have a deal?"

It didn't take long for Tanner to weigh his options. He didn't have any bargaining power here; the few chips that he'd brought to the table were all stripped away, except for one. Alicia knew that she needed his expertise. That was the only reason why he was still in her office, why she hadn't thrown him out on his ass. She needed his insider knowledge, but he needed to get close to her. He suspected that she knew he would keep on trying to bring her down - but if he backed off now, he'd certainly never get another chance.

"It seems that I don't have much of a choice," he admitted wryly.

"Oh, you've always got a choice," she replied immediately, smiling at him. Dammit, he thought, she really even had a nice smile. The kind of smile he could get used to seeing, if it wasn't attached to such a smart and calculating mind. "But in this case, at least, I think that you made the right one."

Without waiting for him to respond to that comment, she pushed back her chair and rose to her feet, flipping closed a leather folder that lay in front of her. "Now, come along," she said, stepping out from behind the desk and heading off towards the door.

Tanner rose to his feet and moved after her, annoyed that she'd seized control of the situation so firmly, but not sure what else to do. This whole "seeing right through him" thing had really knocked his mind for a loop, and he kept feeling off balance, like he was trying to stand on one foot and not fall over.

"Where are we going?" he asked, after a minute of walking.

"I've got a meeting with some of the senior Democrats, discussing the rough draft of my education bill," she called back over her shoulder, not slowing down as they left her office and cut through her staff area. "And since I barely know any of them, I figured that I'd bring you along and see if you can help me out."

"Great. And what exactly am I supposed to do to help out?" He saw Duecent glaring at him as he passed out of the offices, following after Alicia like a dog trailing behind its owner. *Great. Duecent, you don't know the half of it.*

He tried to get his mind back on track. Alicia said she was meeting with some senior Democrats? This seemed like the perfect place to try and kill Alicia's bill, rather than advance it - in her own party - but Tanner gloomily suspected that the woman had already foreseen this possibility, and knew how to counter it.

Alicia turned and beamed at him. "Think of this as the real interview," she suggested, her eyes practically laughing at him, mocking him. "If you help me get through this, I'll keep you around, and not announce that you're the biggest scumbag in Washington since Joseph McCarthy left."

She really was playing with him! Tanner fought furiously to keep his face neutral, while inside he gritted his teeth and imagined himself shoving her down a flight of stairs.

Instead, he held back, trying to think as quickly as he could as he followed Alicia into a meeting room. Sure enough, Senator Harrison Reed himself was there, along with half a dozen other senior Democrats that Tanner recognized. He hadn't blackmailed or otherwise faced off against any of these men, but he knew most of them - or people on their staff teams. He took a seat slightly behind Alicia and hoped that she wouldn't call on him.

As the other politicians and their staff were filtering in, however, Alicia turned back to face him. "So, give me the details on them," she whispered.

Tanner just raised his eyebrows at her. She wanted to use him? That didn't mean that he had to put up with her demanding information from him, like he was some kind of flunky.

Observing his intentions, Alicia made a show out of rolling her blue-green eyes at him. "Oh, get off your damn high horse," she hissed at him. "This is your chance to change my mind about you, remember? Just tell me what things I really ought to know for this meeting, and prove that you're more than just a barracuda in a three thousand dollar suit."

"Fine," Tanner gave in. "Senator Reed has a lot of power to call the shots, but he almost never does. He doesn't like getting caught in anything that ruins his image as a bipartisan leader. Not that he's actually useful for bipartisan negotiations, since he folds like a cheap suit whenever his precious integrity is threatened."

He saw Alicia nod, and kept on moving his eyes around the room. "Okay, coming in now is Nick Durlin, from Illinois. He's basically Reed's opposite - he's a firebrand, loves to jump on to the latest causes. Really loves getting on national television, always wants to be one of those talking heads on CNN or Fox. Massive ego."

Alicia nodded. "Okay, this is good. I can use this."

At least she didn't ask Tanner if he was sure. He

appreciated that confidence, at least. "And the guy sitting in the corner over there is Tom Carp. He doesn't get out much, not super active. Tends to just go with the flow; convince him that the rest of the Party is on board with whatever you propose, and he'll fall in line."

Another nod. Unlike some Senators, who were great at giving the impression that they were listening without actually absorbing a single word, Alicia really did seem to have committed all this information to memory. "Anything else?"

"Yes, one more thing." He paused for a second, waiting for her full attention. "You haven't seen me in a three thousand dollar suit - and when you do, trust me, it will make an impression." He grinned at her, and for just a second, he thought he saw a little glint of that previous sultry fire in her eyes before she quenched it.

The other senators were now taking their places at the table, and Tanner stopped talking so that Alicia could turn back to the meeting. Sitting back, he tried to ignore the curious eyes from several of the other senators' staff members, resting on him. They recognized him, and were undoubtedly wondering what he was doing here.

"Well, it looks like everyone's here," Alicia began, leaning forward and clapping her hands together. The sound had its intended effect of turning the heads of the other senators, and they listened as she began talking, outlining the broad strokes of her education bill. Tanner settled back, letting the words wash over him, giving every outward appearance of listening closely.

Inside his head, however, he fumed, turning over the last few minutes over and over as he tried to work out where he'd gone wrong. How had his situation, his plans, gone so far astray, so quickly? He'd worked out everything, had a perfect plan.

And then Alicia somehow, inexplicably, saw right through him.

Well, no matter, he tried to tell himself. He could still turn this around. After all, he, Keegan Tanner, was known for his skill. He wasn't going to let some minor setback bring him down. There were a million different ways to kill a bill, and he only needed to find one. He might not have won the first round, but he was a long way from getting knocked out.

He narrowed his eyes slightly at Alicia Stone's back as she talked. He'd find a way to bring her down. One way or another, he'd make sure that she got her comeuppance for leading him on, flirting with him and teasing him.

Alicia Stone would be a worthy opponent, but Keegan Tanner would triumph in the end. He'd focus every waking moment on her, learn every detail about her, come to know her utterly and intimately.

And then, when she least expected it, he would destroy her.

CHAPTER EIGHT

"So," Freddie asked as he gazed over the lip of his pint glass at Tanner, "how's the new assignment going? Haven't talked to you for a few days, and your phone keeps going to voicemail. You and that new senator getting into it, huh?"

He waited, but Tanner didn't respond, didn't even look up. He just sat there, gazing down vacantly into his scotch glass, until Freddie reached over and physically twiddled his fingers in front of his eyes. "Yo, man, wake up. What's going on with you? You've been zoned out all evening."

"Oh, have I? Sorry." Tanner blinked, looking up and shaking his head a little. "Yeah, Alicia. She's driving me crazy, that's what."

"Yeah, I can see that you're off your game." Freddie gave Tanner another chance to respond, but the man had already zoned out again. "Come on, dude, talk to me. I've never seen you hung up this much before. What's the matter, you've developed feelings or something?"

Freddie meant these words as a light-hearted joke, but

Tanner suddenly slammed his fist down on the bar, making him jump a little in surprise. "Hell no!" he burst out. "She's a bitch, too smart by half! I most definitely don't have feelings for her!"

"Whoa, easy!" Freddie held up his hands, as if surrendering. "I was just kidding! But this is the first time all week that I've been able to get ahold of you, much less get you out for a drink. What have you been doing with all this time?"

Before answering, Tanner tossed back the rest of his scotch, grimacing as he swallowed. "She's been running me ragged, that's what I've been doing," he complained. "Setting up meetings, giving her briefs on all the other people she meets with - and then, even though I've briefed her, she still drags me along to half the meetings anyway, where I usually just sit behind her and daydream about how her ass looks out of those damn pencil skirts that she always wears. And on top of that, her so-called Chief of Staff, Duecent? Totally incompetent. So now I'm stuck trying to basically single-handedly whip her damn office into shape and hire some people who can tell their heads from their asses." He sighed. "And now I need another drink, because I don't know when the next time I'll even be able to get out of there on time will be."

"Sounds rough," Freddie said sympathetically.

Tanner groaned. "You have no idea. But that damn woman is the worst problem of all. She's in my head now."

"In your head?" Freddie watched, concerned, as Tanner proceeded to lay that very head down on the bar, as if he was about to fall asleep. The man was going to get his suit lapels dirty with the stale beer that constantly coated the railing of the bar, if he wasn't careful. Freddie had never seen Tanner show such a lack of care for his overpriced clothing.

Tanner didn't appear to notice the sticky residue dangerously close to his expensive clothes. "How did she see right through me?" he asked rhetorically. "I totally thought that I had her charmed, eating out of the palm of my hand, ready to snap me up - and instead, she turns the tables on me, like a magician doing that damn trick where he pulls the tablecloth out from underneath all the wine glasses."

Freddie took another pull of his beer as he tried to think of how to respond. He had much less experience with women than Tanner, and he considered the irony of the situation; normally, he would be the one feeling hopeless and asking for advice from Tanner, instead of the other way around.

"Maybe you just need to get out there and distract yourself," he suggested. "It sounds like this Alicia woman has gotten into your head; if you went out and found a different girl to distract yourself, maybe you won't be as bothered by her?"

He wasn't sure if this was actually good advice, but it at least made Tanner sit up. "Actually, that's not bad," the other man replied. "Show myself that I've still got it, that it's Alicia, not me, that's off. Yeah, I can do that!" The bartender came by, pointing at Tanner's glass and raising his eyebrows, and Tanner gave him an enthusiastic nod. "Yes, another!"

Fresh scotch in hand, Tanner spun around on his seat, out to face the crowd. The Capitol Lounge was rapidly filling up with staffers and other young denizens of DC as they came out to whet their whistles and forget about the stress of the day. Tanner ran his eyes over the crowd, surveying the young women like a hungry predator searching for his prey.

"Those two are cute," Freddie volunteered, pointing out two young women who'd just sauntered in, looking around for an open spot. The taller girl was a wispy blonde, while the shorter was a stacked redhead.

"Perfect," Tanner said, perhaps a little too forcefully.

He stood up, looking over at the women. "Hey, need a spot?" he called out loudly.

Freddie winced, but the girls smiled after getting a single look at Tanner's strong, powerful features. They made their way across the crowded bar, over to Tanner and Freddie.

"Hello there!" Tanner greeted the two girls. "I'm Keegan, and this is my buddy Freddie. Care for a drink?"

"Sure!" the redhead exclaimed, the blonde echoing this sentiment with a nod. "Are you two guys in politics?"

The outright, upfront question seemed to throw Tanner for a moment, so Freddie cleared his throat and spoke up. "Actually, Tanner - sorry, Keegan - is working for Senator Stone," he filled in. "And I'm in IT for some of the Congressional buildings. How about you two?"

The blonde hesitantly volunteered that she worked at a nearby coffee shop, while the redhead dove into a story about how she helped work in an office for a congressman, but she didn't want to "name-drop" and reveal her employer. Freddie did his best to nod along, but his occasional glances over at Tanner revealed that his buddy still looked distracted, barely paying attention.

Still, they supplied the girls with a few drinks, and soon the blonde was leaning up against Freddie. With a rush of adrenaline, he slipped his arm around her waist, and was intensely gratified to feel her slide in comfortably against his crotch. "Hi," she murmured down to him, looking over her shoulder and back at him; she stood a good three or four inches taller than him, but he wasn't put off in the slightest.

"Hi, yourself," he murmured back, trying to not psych himself out over what might come next. He could manage this, he prayed; he wouldn't screw it up, as was sadly his par for the course. "Having a good time?"

"I am - but your friend looks a little flustered," she commented back after a minute, flicking her eyes over towards Tanner.

Sure enough, Tanner appeared to have once again tuned out of the conversation. Freddie reached over and poked him. "Hey!" he hissed. "Focus, man!"

With a little shake, Tanner snapped back to the present. Fortunately, the redhead was still halfway through a convoluted story about a very complex coffee run, and hadn't noticed his momentary lapse. "So can you believe that they didn't even have the syrup?" she finished, looking up at Tanner expectantly.

He obediently laughed on the right cue, and Freddie felt a little surge of hope. "So, shall we maybe head out, find someplace a little quieter?" he suggested, nervous energy rushing through him. This was it! Make or break moment!

The blonde turned and looked down at him, and for a timeless second, Freddie held his breath. He quickly repeated her name - Cristina, Cristina, Cristina - inside his head to make sure that he didn't forget, didn't call her by the wrong name.

"Yeah," she finally said, a soft little smile spreading across her fine features. "I'd like that."

Tanner didn't say anything, but he followed along as Freddie, Cristina, and the redhead - whose name Freddie hadn't managed to catch - left the bar. By the time they reached outside, Cristina was hanging off of Freddie in a wonderfully soft manner, and he couldn't think of anything but wanting to get her back to his apartment, as soon as possible, before this miraculous streak of good luck took a turn for the worse.

"I think our paths might part ways here," he said loudly to Tanner, trying to keep the man from losing focus yet again. "You going to be okay?"

"What? Yeah, yeah, I've got this." Tanner blinked, and then looked down at the redhead, who had practically wrapped herself around him. Her low-cut top and massive tits seemed to finally catch his eye, and he smiled. "Hi there, sexy."

"Hi yourself, you big man," the redhead fired back. "How about you take me back to your place, let me see if I can shimmy up you like a tree?"

Freddie nearly choked, quickly covering up the gasp with a bout of coughing. "No, no, I'm fine," he reassured Cristina. How the hell did Tanner find these girls, ones willing to be so open with their sexual desire for him?

With a few taps of his smartphone, Freddie summoned a nearby Uber. "After you," he said to Cristina, still scarcely able to believe his luck as the willowy blonde climbed into the car ahead of him. He couldn't help checking out her ass, marveling that this woman was considering his out-of-shape, slightly chubby body to be a catch, even while standing next to Tanner in a very unflattering comparison.

Before climbing into the car after Cristina, however, Freddie held back for a second longer, giving Tanner a light punch in the shoulder. "Distraction, remember?" he repeated to his best friend.

Tanner nodded, his eyes still lingering on the stacked, short girl clinging to him like he was a life raft. "Right. Distraction." Freddie wished that Tanner sounded a bit more confident, but in the end, what else could he do?

Leaving Tanner and the redhead behind, Freddie climbed into the back of the Uber along with Cristina, leaning forward to confirm his address with the driver. He glanced back one more time at Tanner as the car pulled away, but then Cristina wrapped her arms around him and drew his lips to her own, and he forgot about anything beyond the confines of the vehicle.

The next few hours passed in a blissful haze for Freddie. His apartment wasn't anything special - especially not compared to the massive luxury apartment that Tanner owned - but it was still big enough to make Cristina's eyes gleam, and inspire another round of kissing. He showed her the bedroom, and she peeled off her clothes and gently, almost shyly led him over to the horizontal surface. His movements in bed with her were cautious, almost shy at first, but her kisses and moans buoyed his confidence, and both of them wore huge smiles when, panting, they both finally dropped back to land on top of the tangled sheets.

"Wow," Cristina murmured, pressing herself up against Freddie's warm, soft body. He slid his hand over her torso, curling it possessively around her pert little ass, and she wormed in a bit closer to him.

Only then, their exertions finished, did he hear a faint buzzing sound. "What's that?" he asked, sitting up.

Cristina sighed. "My phone," she replied in her soft, breezy voice. "Vicki keeps on texting me. I've been ignoring her, hoping that she'd take the hint, but she doesn't seem to get it."

Vicki. That must have been the redhead's name. "What's she texting about?" Freddie asked, his heart sinking. If the girl's fingers were moving on her phone, that meant that she wasn't being distracted by Tanner's body and attentions.

"I'm not sure. Let me check." Cristina wiggled off of the bed, and Freddie was momentarily struck dumb as he watched her long body undulate. He could watch that sort of motion forever.

A moment later, Cristina flopped back down beside him in bed, holding her phone. "I guess your friend was a bit of an ass," she said, scrolling through the missed messages. There were a lot of them, Freddie noted gloomily. "He kept on tuning out, and she eventually noticed. She asked him what was wrong, and he called her by some other woman's name!"

"Let me guess," Freddie said, pressing his palm up against his forehead. "He called her Alicia."

Cristina sat up a little more. "Yeah, how did you

know? Oh my god, is he dating someone?"

"No, no, nothing like that!" Freddie corrected quickly. He sighed. "But that's his boss at work, and he's been really over-taxed lately. Tell your friend I'm sorry, okay?"

Cristina texted the apology to Vicki, but then sank back against Freddie. "Told her. And now, I'm turning my phone off for the rest of the night." She smiled up at Freddie. "You'll just have to keep me entertained instead."

"I can handle that," Freddie answered, his heart leaping as thoughts of Tanner fled his mind. Tanner might be having issues, but with a sudden surge of selfishness, Freddie decided that his best friend would just have to fend for himself.

CHAPTER NINE

Okay, Tanner decided with a growl of irritation as he dabbed at the little nick in his face, lowering his razor and setting it down on the side of his bathroom sink. He really needed to do something to change his situation.

After that girl from the bar last night (what was her name... Nicki?) went storming off, yelling about how he wasn't paying attention to her, Tanner decided to instead focus all his attention on the remaining liquid in a vodka bottle sitting in his freezer. Mixed with a splash of vermouth, it wasn't awful, especially after he forced down the first glass and made himself a second one.

Now, however, he had a splitting headache to add to his other problems. And none of this was helping him move any closer to his real goal - killing that damn education bill.

Tanner looked up at his face in the mirror, picking up his razor once again to finish shaving the other half of his chin. He looked drawn and somewhat haggard in the mirror, he thought to himself. Previously, he'd been full of confidence - but in a matter of days, Alicia Stone managed to take that away from him.

He needed to take it back from her.

Maybe it was time for him to act more like his true self, to drop the persona that he'd put on to try and land this job in Alicia's office. After all, she'd seen right through his persona. No reason to keep it going.

Carefully, buoyed by this idea, Tanner finished shaving. He rubbed one hand along his smooth cheek, nodding. Not bad. He then headed for his closet, where, instead of putting on the baggy, cheaper, coffee-stained suit, he grabbed one of his favorites. The Armani cut and custom tailoring had set him back a pretty penny, but he loved the fit, how it sat on his body as if custom molded to him - which, in a way, it was.

Even putting on the expensive suit gave Tanner a boost of confidence. He added a faint little hint of cologne, a perfectly tied knot in the red silk tie at his throat, and pulled on his jacket. There. Already, he felt better. He paused in the kitchen just long enough to make himself a single cup of coffee, downed it, and headed out.

As soon as he walked into Senator Stone's office, Tanner felt more eyes land on him. Sure, he'd been spending most of his days there over the last week, but he'd been ill-dressed, nondescript, just another one of the little pawns who ran around like chickens with their heads cut off as they tried to carry out whatever inane command Alicia, or that idiot Duecent, had given out. Tanner had looked like them, another little servant to bend his knee and scurry.

Now, however, he carried the aura of power, of control. Tanner held his head high, let a little smirk play about his lips, as he crossed the open area of desks and proceeded straight into Alicia's office.

As usual, the woman already sat behind her desk, reading over some bill or report. A tiny little part of Tanner did have to admire her dedication, the hours she put in on the job. Most senators, even in their freshman year, quickly learned that they'd never be able to stay on top of the mountain of paperwork that came along with their seat, and soon abandoned the reading to other flunkies while they snuck in a quick nine on a nearby golf course, usually joined by a few enterprising lobbyists and the girl that drove the beer cart.

Alicia, however, didn't appear ready to take that easy way out of her job. She looked up at him as he entered, her face betraying no indication that she noticed the change in his wardrobe, his attitude.

"Ah, Mr. Tanner, good morning," she greeted him evenly.

"Please, just call me Tanner," he replied. "No need for formality, Senator Stone." He drew out her name a little, and was pleased to see the ghost of a smile dart very briefly about her lips before being squashed and put away.

"Very well, Tanner," she said after a second, nodding to the chair in front of her desk. "We've got a busy day, as usual."

Tanner dropped into the indicated chair, leaning back to affect an attitude of relaxation. He picked up the folder that Alicia passed across to him and leafed briefly through it. Notes on other senators - their recent voting records, stated positions, which lobbyists and companies had contributed recently to their campaigns. Basic stuff, the kind of thing that he already had memorized in his head.

Alicia turned back to her own papers, but glanced up after a minute or two of silence. "You're not reading, Tanner."

Tanner shrugged. "No need. Look, I know all of this stuff, and I also know that poring over it isn't going to get us anywhere. Come on, I've seen your speeches as you ran for election - you know that just reciting dry facts isn't enough to win the support we need. You need energy, drive - and that doesn't come from memorizing which company helped to fund Senator Carp's last reelection."

Across the desk from him, Alicia raised one eyebrow. "And let me guess. You're suggesting that perhaps we go out for a round of golf, maybe head to a strip club where I can have a one on one talk with my constituents?"

He'd noticed her wry sense of humor before in the occasional little remark, but this was the first time she'd directed a joke at Tanner, and he laughed out loud before he could catch himself. "Don't forget to throw in the meal with a few lobbyists, where you kindly allow them to pay for the massive porterhouse steak you order," he added, and felt a little tingle of warmth as he saw Alicia's smile grow a bit wider.

"Of course, how could I forget?" She held a hand against her chest, briefly looking down. "Forgive me, Tanner, I'm still new to this."

"No need to feel too guilty," Tanner fired back, watching as Alicia stood up and stepped around her desk, over to sink down into the chair next to him.

"But I do feel guilty," she insisted, batting long eyelashes at him. She really did have nice eyes, he couldn't help noticing. "I'm just a bumpkin from the sticks, somehow elected to this position where I'm totally in over my head, and I need a wise, experienced, strong man to lean on, someone who can guide me, show me the ropes…"

It took Tanner a second to realize that Alicia was leaning forward, once again daring him to betray himself by flicking his eyes to her cleavage, those big blue-green eyes threatening to drown him. She was pulling the fake seduction card again - but this time, he recognized it, was ready for it.

"I can be that man for you, big and strong," he murmured back to her. This time, he left no illusion about the long, considering look that he aimed down her shirt, examining her chest before rising back up to her face. Really, not an unpleasant sight in the slightest, he thought to himself, nearly distracting himself from his own words. "But I'll need something in response from you. Your integrity, your self-respect - and probably that hot body of yours, too."

His smile grew as Alicia's eyes widened in surprise. "Excuse me?" she started, a flush of heat entering her cheeks.

Tanner kept leaning forward and holding her heated gaze for another second longer. "Come on, what do you say? You and me, right here on your desk, in full view of your office? That should teach them the reward for hard work. I probably won't put in my top effort, but I'm sure you won't notice, given how you're starved for sex."

He somehow kept his face straight for another second as her eyes grew even wider, her mouth slipping in slack-jawed speechlessness - and then sat back, grinning widely, feeling a bit like a schoolboy who'd just managed to sneak his first kiss. "Hey, you want to tease me, you best be prepared to get it thrown back at you."

The look of surprise on her face, her mouth dropping wide open, gratified him more than he'd anticipated.

Still, Alicia quickly pulled herself back under control. "You know, Tanner, talking to me like that is definitely enough to get you fired," she pointed out, rising to her feet. "And if I fire you, well, I just might be asked to explain to my colleagues exactly what I disliked about you, why I had to let you go." She shrugged. "You know how gossip spreads in a town like this one."

"But you can't fire me," Tanner countered, also standing up. Alicia was tall, he noted, but he still had almost two inches on her. He used that extra height to his advantage, looking down at her as he took a step forward.

"And why not?" She didn't back away, even as he loomed over her.

"Because you need me, just as much as I need to preserve my own reputation." Tanner didn't know if this was the truth, but it was the only conclusion he'd reached this morning that made sense, and it felt right to his gut intuition. "You're new here, out of your depth. Despite your attitude, this aura of competence that you project, you know that you need my help if you want this bill to have any shot in Hell of passing. If you fire me, you'll be dooming yourself."

He'd drawn closer to Alicia as he spoke, and now stood less than a foot from her. He could practically feel the heat of her body, could look down into her face and see those big, green-blue eyes moving back and forth across his own features as she tried to determine whether he was bluffing. He kept his own face clear, not giving out any hints. He'd played this game before. He knew how to hold a poker face.

She drew a deep breath. Tanner felt, rather than saw, her chest rise; even her well-tailored blouse couldn't contain the raw biology beneath it. Strangely, he felt an answering surge of warmth course through him, the heat of raw, primal attraction, but he pushed that sensation off to the side. Instead, he waited, knowing that he could outlast her.

And then, after an eternity of silence, she blinked.

"Very well," she said quietly, her tone barely above a whisper. "You're right. I do need your help. We both need each other."

"Glad to hear you admit it," Tanner answered. In the back of his mind, a little part of him noted that hearing Alicia say those words sent another little rush of warmth through him. Why? He ignored it. Probably just pent-up frustration with her, not finding any other outlet in his head except through the suggestion of sex.

Whoops. Don't think about sex. It had been at least a full week since the last time Tanner had a girl - an eternity, in his life - and he felt an uncomfortable stiffening. Push it down, don't let that come up now, he commanded himself. Think soft thoughts.

"Listen," he said to Alicia, wanting to diffuse the tension still sparking between them. "Let's go out, get some coffee, chat for a little while before your meetings start. We can talk about strategies for selling the bill, some emotional hooks that you can use, ways to really show your passion for this."

Alicia started to nod, but stopped. "No can do - my first meeting's in just a few minutes," she said, glancing down at the delicate watch on her wrist. Tanner's eyes moved along with hers, downward, and he caught another quick little glimpse down her blouse, catching the swell of her breasts. Shit. He closed his eyes, trying to think of anything non-sexual, anything neutral. Coffee. Biscuits. Milk - no, where did milk come from, that wasn't helping-

"But I'm free tonight," Alicia went on, looking back up at him. Just in time, he drew his eyes off of her breasts as they nestled together inside that tight blouse, back to her face. "Maybe we could plan out some possible speech topics over dinner?"

"Yes, that sounds good," Tanner replied quickly. He could work with dinner. What was important was that he was a part of these speeches, that he knew every step of the Stone campaign before it happened - so that he could plan out a countermove. "I'll pick the place, get us reservations. Let's say, around seven?"

"Perfect," Alicia answered. "Seven."

Tanner expected her to turn away, gather her notes and head off to her first meeting of the morning. Instead, however, he saw Alicia hesitate for a fraction of a second longer, looking up at him. Those faintly red patches of heat in her cheeks suddenly flared up again, just before she turned away.

Previously, that heat was from anger, from him countering her little verbal ploy, her fake seduction. But why did they flare up again? Tanner briefly frowned. Was she angry at even the idea of having dinner with such a slippery individual as himself?

Or - and he hesitated even to consider this option - was that heat not from anger after all? Was there something else there?

Interesting, Tanner noted to himself, turning as he watched Alicia head out of her office, stack of papers in hand. He had no guarantee that there was any sort of real attraction there - but if there was, that was something he could use.

Idly, his eyes dropped down to watch Alicia's ass, tight in that sexy little pencil skirt, as she left the office. Already, he couldn't even count how many times he'd pictured her naked, unable to talk as she moaned from him plunging himself into her, replacing all those annoying orders with moans and gasps of pleasure as he took her-

He sighed after the door closed. Judging from the hard-on in his pants, he really needed to get laid, and soon. He was so desperate, he was even finding bitchy, controlling Alicia Stone to be attractive.

CHAPTER TEN

After some consideration, Tanner placed a call to Bayou, a Cajun high-end restaurant located in the West End neighborhood. He gave his name, confirmed that he needed a table for two at seven, and ended the call after receiving the host's assurances that they'd save the best table for the Senator and himself.

The rest of the day passed quickly, Tanner looking ahead already to the evening. He needed to get Alicia to open up, let down her shields around him, he decided. He needed her to see him as a trustworthy confidante, someone with whom she felt comfortable revealing the inner workings of her plans, her next steps in pushing the education bill.

He needed, he reminded himself as he arrived five minutes early at the restaurant, to be smooth, charming, attentive - and above all else, a good listener.

Tanner strolled up to the entrance to Bayou, expecting to be the first one to arrive and planning to check in - elected politicians never arrived anywhere on time. It was like a genetic disorder with them, one he'd come to expect.

But when he reached the host's station, the man smiled at him and picked up two menus.

"Ah, Mr. Tanner," the host greeted him with a smile. "If you'll follow me?"

Tanner frowned, but moved after the host as he weaved his way through the narrow wooden tables, past the booths upholstered in red leather. They headed over to Tanner's favorite table, one set just far back enough from the window to let him look out at the passing pedestrians outside, but not so close that someone might spot his face and recognize him through the window.

And there, already sitting in one of the two seats, was Senator Alicia Stone, sipping slowly on a glass of something dark with a single ice cube floating in it.

For a moment, Tanner froze, his mind going blank with surprise. Alicia was here early, getting to the table before him? He recovered quickly, his face returning to its pleasant smile with astounding rapidity, but she had to have seen that brief look of concern.

"Sorry, but I hate being that person who shows up late," Alicia said as Tanner slid into the booth across from her, not sounding sorry in the slightest.

"Well, that certainly makes you different from most of the other legislators I work with," Tanner replied, looking back at her across the table. The waiter bobbed near their table, and he ordered his usual, Laphroaig 25.

"Not bad," Alicia commented, as the waiter turned and darted away to bring him his request. "A bit overdone."

"What, my scotch choice?" Tanner replied, his eyes moving to Alicia's glass. "And here I was, taking you for a vodka and cranberry girl."

She raised her eyebrows at him, a curiously alluring taunt. "And what does that imply, exactly?"

"I have absolutely no idea," Tanner countered, keeping his face completely straight. If she wanted to exchange volleys of taunts, well, he could return just as well as serve. "I don't believe that a cocktail implies anything about the person."

Alicia chuckled. "Rich, coming from the man who orders a splash out of a four hundred dollar bottle of scotch. That's not trying to say anything?"

This time, it was Tanner's turn to raise his eyebrows. "All it implies," he said innocently as the waiter set his drink in front of him, "is that I enjoy a good scotch."

Round one ends in a draw, Tanner thought to himself as the two of them eyed each other, both taking a moment to nip at the smooth, well-aged liquor. Round two will begin momentarily.

The silence, however, persisted even after the waiter stopped by and collected their orders (Alicia went for the jambalaya, while Tanner elected to go with the crawfish étouffée). They both just watched each other across the table, waiting for the other to make a move.

As he sat there, however, Tanner's thoughts started to stray. His eyes drifted over Alicia's outfit, noting that it was quite a bit snugger than her usual work ensembles. She certainly didn't need to worry about anyone mocking her for being out of shape, he noted with a grudging flare of admiration. Those tight clothes revealed an absolute knockout of a body, tight and trim in all the right places, plump and wonderfully soft in others. If she wasn't who she was, he'd already be thinking ahead to peeling that cute little dress-up outfit off of her, bending her over his couch and moving up against her from behind-

At least, he would have done this if she wasn't who she was, he reminded himself. But who she was - a senator, a Democrat, a target - made her his enemy.

Still, he couldn't completely fight off those tempting little daydreaming images that flitted through his head, suggesting many better ways that they could spend the end of the evening together.

Their food arrived, and Alicia finally broke the silence. "We're really getting a lot accomplished here, aren't we?" she remarked, her voice heavy with sarcasm.

For a moment before answering, Tanner examined this sentence for verbal snares or traps, but his search came up empty. "Yeah, this perhaps won't be as productive as I imagined," he admitted, matching her wry tone.

Alicia sighed. "Look, I get it. You see me as the enemy, and I don't trust you as far as I could throw you." She flexed her bare arms, revealing trim and fit muscles. "Which is still further than you'd suspect," she added with a little smirk.

"So what are you suggesting that we do? It seems like we're stuck at an impasse."

She considered this for a moment while delicately eating a mouthful of dirty rice. "What about a truce?" she finally suggested.

Tanner frowned. This seemed too straightforward. "A truce?"

"Sure - I'll stop taunting you, and you'll stop actively plotting to undermine me." Alicia laughed. "Of course, we both know what will happen when the end date of the truce comes along, but we can work together until then. Our end goals might be opposed, but we can still help each other in the short term and both come out ahead."

Tanner took a bite of his étouffée as he considered the advantages and possible downsides. It was true that, if they kept on keeping their shields up and firing exchanges back and forth, neither of them would make much progress. Instead of killing Alicia's education bill, he'd instead be leaving it up to chance - a coin flip.

Those odds weren't enough for Tanner to risk his reputation on it.

"Very well," he finally said, shaking his head a little, surprised that he was agreeing with this unexpected direction. "A truce. And what are the details?"

Alicia pursed her lips, tapping her fork idly against her bowl as she considered. With her lips pouting like that, Tanner couldn't help but feel another little rush of hunger for her, one that had nothing to do with the delicious food in front of him. He quickly ate another bite of crawfish to cover up any sign of his arousal.

"Two weeks," she said finally. "That's enough time for us to get the bill in place, but you can still have a few days to try and bring it down. I will, of course, be trying to stop you, but you can try."

"Two weeks," Tanner repeated.

Alicia nodded. "And during that time, we're on the same side. You're on my side, and you're being helpful. No false personas, no trying to lead me down the wrong avenue, no giving me the wrong information, nothing like that."

"And what do I get?" Tanner asked.

"You?" Alicia blinked. "You get me being honest with you."

Tanner sat back and considered his options, covering by taking another sip of his scotch. It wasn't an ideal situation, but this whole thing with Alicia had been on the wrong foot since the beginning. He'd spent the whole time off balance, with her somehow, inexplicably, managing to keep one step ahead of him. He hated to admit it, but he needed this truce, perhaps even more than she did.

"Honesty," he said, drawing out the word, tasting it as if he'd never encountered it before. "This might be new for me."

Alicia actually snorted, a short little laugh that she couldn't fully contain. "Maybe it will help you grow, make you a little less of an ass," she countered.

"Low blow," Tanner protested. But after another second, he set his drink down and held his hand across the table, careful not to let his sleeve dip into his entree. "But I don't see any other options. Deal."

"Deal," Alicia agreed, shaking his offered hand.

"So, care to tell me everything?" Tanner cracked, after taking his hand back.

Alicia, however, didn't laugh. "Where would you like me to start?"

Tanner searched his mind. What sort of question would give him a hint at her weaknesses, would offer a crack in her armor that he could exploit later? He tried to find the most strategic question possible to ask - but instead, his mouth chose an entirely different question, one that he hadn't even considered asking.

"Why didn't you get that spot as high school valedictorian?"

Across from him, Alicia blinked; clearly, that wasn't the question she'd been expecting. "That's what you want to know?" she exclaimed.

Tanner hadn't intended to ask that question, but he realized that he truly did feel curious. "Yes, it is."

She blinked at him, rearranging her thoughts. "It was my own fault," she said at length. "I had a class with a teacher who really liked me, because I was the model student."

"Somehow, I can see that," Tanner commented, making her smile.

"Well, I thought that, since the teacher really liked me, I could breeze past the final in the class. I didn't study, didn't put in the time - and I totally bombed it." Even now, Tanner saw a wince pass across Alicia's face at the memory. "I went to the teacher, begged him to let me retake the exam, but he stayed firm. He told me that I'd be fine, still have the future I wanted - but I needed this as a lesson to show me that I needed to work at being perfect."

"It seemed to have worked," Tanner said, trying to keep her from getting depressed. Her face had fallen as she remembered that particular moment in her past.

She sighed, but then brightened again. "It did, I

suppose. I didn't agree with him at the time, but I suppose that I do now - not that I'd want him to do it again, if I had the chance!"

That first question seemed to break the dam. "Now, your turn," Alicia told Tanner. "What did you want to be as a kid, before you sold your soul to the Republican party?"

"First off, they paid a very nice premium for that soul, and it's proved to be a far better investment than any other that I've made," Tanner countered. He thought back, seeking a truthful answer. "But when I was younger, I really did want to go into politics. I still believed that it was pure, that I could do real good, that it wasn't all just another system to be manipulated."

"So cynical," Alicia murmured, shaking her head at him. "I hope I never get like that."

She likely didn't mean for the words to sting, but they did. Tanner didn't let it show, but he winced inside. "Trust me, you'll either get kicked out of Washington, or you'll come around to my way of thinking real soon. It's just how things work around here. No way around it."

But Alicia remained resolute. "Maybe," she admitted. "But it doesn't have to keep on being that way forever."

After a second of quiet, however, she shook off her pensiveness. "Okay, your turn for a question," she said, taking the opportunity to grab another bite of food.

Tanner pursed his lips at her as he watched her chew, and then blot her lips with a napkin. "First high school boyfriend," he said.

Alicia coughed, quickly grabbing for her glass of water. "What??"

"You heard me," he said, grinning despite himself, glad to have unseated her composure. "Name, what he did to land you, and how far you went with him."

"You can't be serious."

Tanner leaned forward, fighting to keep his face blank.

"You did say that you wanted this truce, and you'd be open and honest. If you can't answer a simple question like this, I might have to think about revoking my services-"

"Oh, knock it off, you ass," Alicia cut him off, but she was smiling as she did so. "Fine. My first boyfriend was probably Harvey Dylan, way back in sixth grade, and he got me by finding a frog on the playground and trying to shove it…"

CHAPTER ELEVEN

"I suppose that I probably ought to be getting home," Alicia said, several hours later, finally glancing down at her watch. She blinked, rubbed her eyes, held the watch face up a little closer. "Wow, is it really that late already?"

"Time flies," Tanner commented across the table, stifling a comfortable little burp. After a rocky start, he'd actually had quite a fun night, he had to admit! He kept on needling Alicia with personal questions, hoping to embarrass her, but to his surprise, she kept on answering! He felt his grudging respect for her continuing to grow. She might already be regretting the deal that she'd struck with him, but she was sticking to her word.

"What, are you having fun?" Alicia asked, gasping and holding one hand to her mouth in mock surprise. "Impossible!"

"Oh, come on. You've been having fun, too," Tanner replied, stretching his hands above his head. "I saw you grinning at some of those questions that you asked me. How in the world could knowing what kind of underwear I wear help you better understand me?"

"Just trying to get in your head, that's all," Alicia said merrily.

"My head? That wasn't the part that I thought you were trying to get into."

Laughing, Alicia smacked him lightly in the arm. "Here, let's get going. I need to get to bed at some point, you know, or I'm going to be absolutely useless tomorrow."

"Is that an invitation?" The words slipped out of Tanner's mouth, helped by the three scotches he'd ended up consuming, before he could consider the implication.

Alicia just laughed, but looking across the table at her, Tanner swore that he saw that flush creep momentarily back up into her cheeks. Maybe there really was something there, after all.

Tanner paid for dinner, over Alicia's brief objections, and then they headed out of the restaurant. The chill of DC's night air made Alicia shiver, and she leaned in against Tanner.

"Here," he said, pulling off his suit coat and draping it around her shoulders.

"You really don't need to-"

"Oh, just take it," he interrupted, smiling. "I dislike seeing a woman shiver, even if that woman happens to be my mortal enemy."

"Mortal enemy? I'm so honored," Alicia cracked, but she kept the jacket.

Outside, she looked around, and then gestured with her thumb over her shoulder. "I actually walked here - my apartment's not too far away. So I'll see you tomorrow-"

"Nonsense," Tanner cut in. "You walked here? And you're going to walk back? Alone, in DC, at night?"

Alicia smiled at him, slipping one hand into her purse. "Trust me, I can handle myself."

"Still not happening," Tanner insisted. Not waiting to see what she pulled out of her purse, he turned and stepped up alongside her. "I'm walking you home. And besides," he added before she could protest, "I'm doing it mainly because I want to get my jacket back. You wouldn't believe what I paid for that, and I can see you deciding to put it through a shredder or something, just to get back at me."

"Ass," Alicia muttered, but she didn't turn him down. Instead, as they started off down the sidewalk together, she slipped her arm through Tanner's.

He nearly jumped at the little electric shock that transferred from the bare skin of her fingers over to his own. He'd been fighting against errant thoughts of touching her, running his hands over her, all night. Now, to have her leaning in comfortably against him… all of those fantasies came roaring back to full life, unable to be silenced inside his head.

Get it together, he snapped at himself, but those voices, those fantasies, only fell silent for a moment before creeping back up. So instead, he just kept his lips pressed tightly together, trying to not let on that he was having distractingly sexy fantasies about this senator, still his enemy - truce or not.

Alicia didn't say anything as they walked along, either. Tanner wondered what she was thinking about, considered asking. But what did he want her to say? What he wanted, he knew that she wouldn't tell him. So he just kept his mouth shut.

They walked down the streets, finally stopping in front of a bank of converted brownstones, rising up three stories, crumbling a little but still elegant and well maintained. "Well, this is home," Alicia commented, fiddling in her purse for her keys.

"Nice place," Tanner remarked, looking up at it. He meant it - this was actually a nice neighborhood, on the up and up, the kind of place where young professionals spent their bonuses, still shocked by how much they made out of college.

"Thanks - moving here was a hassle, but I've finally

got most of it unpacked." Alicia paused for a moment. "Sorry to make you walk."

"No problem," Tanner returned. "Like I said, I'm just here for my jacket."

"Right." Alicia had her keys looped around her finger, but she stepped forward, shrugging her arms out of the jacket.

Tanner also stepped forward, reaching out to lift the jacket off of her shoulders. His hands, however, ended up around Alicia, brushing against the bare skin of her back, exposed as she shrugged out of the jacket.

Both of them froze, another shock of electricity passing between them from the contact with bare skin. This time, looking down into Alicia's eyes, Tanner saw a flare of heat in those cool blue-green irises, and knew immediately that she felt the tingle as well. They both stood there for a moment, looking into each other's eyes, frozen.

Inside Tanner's head, he heard a cacophony of different thoughts, all shouting back and forth - but they all seemed curiously muted, the warm radiance from Alicia's eyes seeming to damp down all of the intrusive thoughts. He couldn't break away, couldn't speak, couldn't do anything at all. He felt like a captive in his own mind.

"Tanner," Alicia murmured, but she didn't pull away. If anything, she leaned in even closer, her chest brushing ever so lightly against his shirt and tie.

Tanner opened his lips slightly, although he had no idea what he would say. He needed to remove himself from this situation, he knew. This was approaching a dangerous line; he'd long since abandoned the idea of seducing Alicia, sensing that she'd be expecting such an obvious move, would defeat any attempt at outright blackmail or intimidation.

He'd just let go of her, step back, and wish her a good night.

Easy. Good plan.

Tanner moved.

He didn't move back, however, didn't let go of Alicia. Instead, his arms tightened around her, drawing her in closer. His jacket slipped off of her shoulders, down to the ground, probably covering itself in dirt and dust.

Tanner didn't notice. Alicia was there, in his arms, not resisting. On the contrary; her eyes sparkled up at him, drawing him in, hypnotic. "Tanner," she whispered again, her voice barely audible.

That little whisper broke his last straw of reserve.

Tanner bent forward, kissed her. He pulled her up against him, feeling the curves of her body press against him. She was supple, yielding, and just the sensation of her warm body nestling in against him enough to set his nerve endings afire. She tasted wet and soft, luscious as her mouth melted against his, and he drank her in like a man lost in a desert stumbling upon a fresh, miraculous oasis.

Dimly, he knew that he shouldn't be doing this. This was wrong; he ought to be letting her go, stepping back, apologizing for crossing the line, backing away before he did any more damage. That was the right thing to do; this, on the other hand, was totally wrong.

He needed to stop.

He didn't stop.

Fireworks went off in his brain, silencing those voices telling him what he should be doing. He couldn't seem to think past the present moment; Alicia was in his arms, her mouth on him, and he needed her. He felt himself throbbing, painfully erect in his pants, more aroused and awake than he'd felt since his first crush at age fifteen had kissed him back. He needed her - his body screamed out for her…

But he finally released her, drawing back his mouth, if not his hands. He opened his mouth to say something, but he didn't have any words.

"This is…" Alicia began, but she stopped, just looking up at him.

"Wrong," Tanner finished, not letting go of her. His hand pressed in against her shoulder, and he could feel her heartbeat, thumping quickly against her ribs, almost like a bird or a small animal.

"We shouldn't…" Again, Alicia seemed to run out of steam before the end of the sentence. Her eyes were locked on him, hungry, drinking him in and mesmerizing him.

She wasn't pulling away, he realized. She kept her own arms around him, holding tightly to him. She shivered up against him, but he suspected that this one had nothing to do with the chill in the night air.

"Inside," Tanner managed to get out, his eyes drifting briefly past her, up to the front door to her brownstone, before returning back to her face, her beautiful features.

Alicia nodded, and her keys clinked in her hand. "Yes. Inside." She turned around, and Tanner barely managed to bend down and grab his jacket off of the ground before dashing up and after her.

Alicia's apartment building featured two doors - the first one granted access to the mailboxes, while the second one led to the actual apartments. Alicia moved towards the second door, but Tanner, his brain afire and filled with nothing but the singing hunger of his raging need, reached out and grabbed her again, once more pulling her to him.

This time, he pushed her back against the wall as he kissed her, pinning her between his body and the row of mailboxes. She eagerly pushed back against him, her hips grinding up against him and nearly making him explode, right then and there! Was it just that he'd gone so long without release? He'd never need a single, particular woman, this woman, so much!

Tanner kissed her lips again, deeply, tasting her with his tongue, and then moved sideways, down, along the graceful slender curve of her neck. Alicia angled her head to give him better access, squirming in his hands - and then, as he nibbled at her collarbone, she moaned.

That soft sound, barely audible, burned away the last little bit of rational thought in Tanner's head.

He spun her around, pointing Alicia towards the second door leading inside. She staggered unsteadily forward, her key bouncing infuriatingly off of the lock half a dozen times before she managed to finally slip it inside. He waited impatiently behind her, his heart thumping like a jackhammer in his chest, awash in unthinking need.

Finally, she had the door open. Tanner followed her upstairs, up to her apartment. She unlocked the door and then, even as her hand reached out for the light switch, he was on her again, kissing, feeling. This time, when she turned and reciprocated, pushing his jacket off of his shoulders and down to fall on her floor, he didn't even give a thought to picking it up, hanging it or draping it on something less dirty.

"The door," Alicia gasped, reaching out for her front door, still open to the hallway.

Tanner stuck out his hand behind him, fumbling about. Finally, frustrated, he tore his eyes away from this woman, the source of this drastic need, just long enough to grab the handle and draw it shut. He reached up and threw the deadbolt across, just for good measure.

Door locked, Tanner turned back to Alicia - and saw that heat rekindled in her eyes, sparkling and alive. She didn't need to say a single word. She raised a finger, crooked it ever so slightly in his direction, and he found himself pulled forward as if on invisible strings.

She backed towards a door as he started forward her. Dimly, Tanner guessed that the bedroom might lie behind that door.

He didn't care. Right now, he just felt his need, burning inside his chest, in his rock-hard cock in his pants, demanding her. He needed to quench it, before it

consumed him.
    He followed after Alicia, driven by need.

CHAPTER TWELVE

Sure enough, the next room in Alicia's apartment was a bedroom. Alicia was on the bed already, her shoes kicked off, her legs disappearing enticingly up into her pencil skirt, that little smirking smile on her face. He wanted to get down on his hands and knees and crawl up that skirt, figuring out where those legs came together.

Tanner looked down at her from the doorway for a second, his blood nearly boiling in his veins. He knew that they were crossing forbidden boundaries, but he needed her, felt practically insane with his hunger.

His hands rose up, fumbling with the buttons on his shirt - but in a flash, Alicia was there, on her knees on the bed, leaning forward to grab at his tie and tug him forward. "My job," she murmured up to him, her voice husky, as her fingers undid each button slowly, revealing a little more of his muscled chest.

Instead, Tanner turned his attention to her outfit. Bit by bit, he peeled her clothes off of her, even as she did the same to him. With each newly exposed square inch of her skin, tanned and gorgeous, he felt his hunger for her grow even stronger. His cock pushed out against his pants, temporarily impeding Alicia's efforts to undo his belt.

He collapsed down on the bed as he finally shook off his pants, his hands pulling her down along with him. She was warm and soft in his arms, a creature of sex and lust. How could anyone listen to this woman when she spoke, think of anything but taking her? Tanner couldn't understand. He had to have her, felt driven to make her moan, come, shudder and release on his spear.

He sank back on the soft covers, Alicia astride him, above him. He'd already popped the clasp on her bra, and her amazing rack now dangled above him. How the hell did she hide these in those classy, professional outfits that she wore? Now freed from their encumbrances, he couldn't believe her figure, her proportions. She was practically a sex doll, alive and moving eagerly in his arms atop him!

Alicia looked down at him, those eyes filled with some emotion that Tanner couldn't quite recognize. He didn't stop, however, didn't ask her what she was thinking. Instead, sitting partially up, he drew her chest against him and explored it with his hands, his lips, his tongue.

"Ohh," he heard her gasp, above him, as he moved across that wonderful rack, feeling her softness in his hands. He found her nipple, ran first his thumb, and then his tongue over it. He felt her stiffen and prickle at his touch, and she arched forward to push him closer.

"More," she commanded, her hands tangling in his hair, mussing it as her fingers knotted inside to pull him closer.

Tanner immediately obeyed. His body vibrated, almost like a taut string on a guitar, as he pushed against her, needing her to press back against him. The touch of her bare skin against his, the gentle brush of her breasts against his face, ignited his core like a flamethrower. He paradoxically wanted both to rush ahead and make her his, and to prolong this, enjoy the sweet agony, for as much time as he could endure.

But Alicia's hands roamed down, finding his hardness, drawing it out of his pants. She held him in her hands, and whatever need Tanner thought he'd felt before was dwarfed by a new rush. With an inarticulate growl rising up from his throat, he threw her to the bed, climbed atop her.

He felt her resistance as he pushed down, but she spread her legs wide, welcoming him in, wanting him. Her skirt was bunched up around her waist, but her panties caught at him, impeding him. With a hiss of frustration, she pulled them off and threw them recklessly aside.

Nothing else stood in his way. Once again, Tanner came down, feeling her push against him, angling up to meet him as he thrusted forward.

Warmth, wetness, a soft and irresistible tightness that still drew him in further. His arms, on either side of Alicia's shoulders, held him inches above her. Her hands came up, wrapping around his neck, sliding down his broad back and drawing him down to her.

Her lips met his, and Tanner thought no more. His body moved against her, feeling her move back in response. This was all that he needed.

They kept in motion together, sometimes growing fiercer, sometimes relaxing. Soon, Tanner felt Alicia's kisses against him grow wilder, less controlled, as her breath came quicker.

"More, faster," she gasped into his ear, and his body instantly obeyed her.

She panted against him, her body flexing with new need as he pumped in and out, long strokes that pushed her closer to that cliff. Tanner saw the fire growing higher in her eyes, almost overtaking her. She tried to fight back against it, hold onto herself, but it was a fight that they both knew she'd lose.

And then, with one last gasp, her body went rigid

beneath him as her orgasm took her.

Tanner slowed, but didn't stop, watching as this woman, normally so controlled and determined and powerful, surrendered herself to emotion and physical sensation. Her eyes rolled back as she went mindless, and she clutched at him, drawing him against her, needing him. He felt her heart beating like a jackrabbit inside her chest as her soft breasts squished against his own body, heard her breath come in ragged panting.

He held her, kissed her, still unable to think but happy that she was happy. She clung to him, a rock in a powerful storm, until her eyes finally blinked and refocused on him.

"Again," she commanded him, those full, gorgeous lips turning up in a ghost of a smile.

He hastened to obey.

When Tanner finally felt his own surge coming on, driving him towards mindlessness, he merely groaned - and Alicia, now on top of him, grinned broadly as she immediately guessed his intentions.

"Yes, give it to me," she insisted, refusing to let him push her off, refusing his attempts to slow down, to delay the train he felt rushing down the tracks towards him. She bent low, her tits dangling in his face and bumping gently against his chin. Her hair fell in waves around his face, closing the two of them off in their own private little world. Further south, her hips rose and fell against him, beating out a primal rhythm against him as she rode his spear, flexing her thighs as they squeezed his body between them.

"God," Tanner gasped out, as the last vestiges of control slipped away. He was no stranger to an orgasm, but he'd never felt one build so much before it hit, come on so strongly. He had a brief mental image of a surfer gazing up at a tidal wave, towering many stories above him.

And then it hit, and Tanner thought of nothing at all as his mind fractured.

She rode him, let him shudder against her, slowed her

motions to a gentle rocking to help him prolong as much as he could. Only when his eyes finally reopened, looking up at her in wonder, did she stop, settling down to press the length of her warm softness against him.

For several minutes, neither of them spoke.

Inside Tanner's head, he couldn't seem to hold on to a thought long enough to see it through to its conclusion. *I just slept with softness, warmth, comfort-*

Try again. I just had sex with Alicia so amazing, so strong an orgasm, never before, need it again-

No, again. Now that we've done this together, she'll certainly believe me when I tell her need to kiss her again, taste her, feel her body come against mine as I make her scream and cry out and want me over and over...

Clearly, sleeping with Alicia had scrambled his brains much more than he'd anticipated.

Next to him, still partially atop him, Alicia blinked, moved a little closer against him as she squirmed to get comfortable. A soft little sound, barely even a sigh, slipped out of her, and Tanner inexplicably felt himself harden a little at even that small, barely audible noise. How could she still have a hold on him, even after he'd just attained release?

Finally, Alicia turned, enough so that she could rest her chin on his broad chest and gaze down into his eyes. "So," she said.

That was it. Just "So." Tanner tried to think, tried to strategize, but his brain felt as if someone had run rampant inside of it, wielding a stick blender with reckless abandon.

"So," he repeated back, aware that he sounded like an idiot but not knowing what else to say.

"That..." Alicia seemed to be experiencing a similar struggle for words. "That wasn't what I expected to happen."

"No, me neither." Was this all that they were capable of? Small talk, as they lay naked together after gloriously coupling in Alicia's bed? Fighting that sluggishness in his mind, Tanner tried to find something, anything else to say. "I promise, I didn't do that because…"

Alicia sat up a little more as Tanner trailed off. "Because of what?" she asked.

He wished he hadn't gone down this path. "Because I want to blackmail you, get leverage over you, anything like that."

He expected her to blow up, to get angry that he'd even consider such a repulsive action. Instead, however, Alicia surprised him by nodding, as if he'd stated that the Earth was round, or that she was currently naked.

"Of course not," she replied, her hand reaching up to brush the side of his face. "Because we're on a truce."

Yes, of course! The truce! Tanner's mind seized onto this explanation like a drowning sailor catching onto a life preserver. Because they were on a truce, his intentions were noble! He didn't sleep with her in an effort to seduce her and blackmail her - he just felt a rush of desire, and she reciprocated! That was all!

As he grabbed onto this flimsy excuse, Alicia sat up in bed, shaking her head slightly to send her hair cascading down her back. "And now, I think that I could use a shower," she announced. She spared one last look down at Tanner's nude body, stretched out on full display, and he saw that little smirk once again dance around her lips as her eyes ran over his bulging biceps, the texture of his six-pack, his muscular thighs. Was she admiring what she'd just conquered? Laughing at how easily she got him into bed? Hungry for more?

By the time that Tanner sat up, his lips trying to form one of the dozen hazy questions buzzing around in his head, Alicia was already out of the room, the bathroom door drifting most of the way closed behind her. Seconds later, Tanner's ears caught the rush of water as the shower started up.

What should he do now? Tanner looked down at himself, still naked, still sweaty, goosebumps beginning to pop out here and there across his skin as the beads of sweat evaporated and carried off some of his body heat. He probably needed to get dressed, head home, get away from Alicia and her ability to scramble his thoughts and see inside his head. There, he could relax, try and figure out just how this ended up happening, how he could use it to his advantage in the developing chess game between the Senator and himself.

He stood up, his hand starting to reach for his pants - but paused, looking over at the door to her bathroom.

It still stood partially open, and he could see little bits of warm mist drifting out. His legs betraying him, Tanner moved closer. Alicia's shower apparently featured sliding glass doors, rather than a curtain - and he could catch the thinnest little glimpse of fresh, flushed pink skin as she moved inside. A soft, melodic hum drifted out through the cracked door.

Was the cracked door an invitation?

Tanner knew that he needed to leave, that staying would only make this worse. But even as his mind agreed that yes, departure was the prudent decision, his legs carried him into the bathroom and his hand reached out to push the shower door open.

Alicia just smiled at him as he slipped inside, her body soft and warm and wet as it pulled him in, her lips already against his own...

CHAPTER THIRTEEN

Back in his own apartment, several hours later, Tanner stared straight ahead at the blackness of his television. He hadn't bothered to turn it on; he knew that he couldn't focus well enough to follow a news or entertainment program at the moment.

What had he done? What had he been thinking?

Well, to be fair, Tanner knew the answer to that second question. He hadn't been thinking, not in any way, shape, or form. He'd walked Alicia back to her apartment after spending the entire evening getting to know her better, acting almost like he was on a date, and yes, fantasizing about how she'd feel in bed, naked and willing beneath him, her hot skin pressed against his own.

Amazing, he sighed, thinking back to their time together in her bed - and then shook his head, reaching up to lightly slap himself across the cheek. Knock it off! Stop dwelling on that!

It was true, however. He'd been fantasizing about her from the moment that he met her. Something about that cool demeanor, the way that she instantly shut him down and saw right through his fake persona, spotted that he wasn't being honest with her, caught his attention in a way that no other woman had managed in the past. That, right from the beginning, drew him to her.

And that body, and the way that she used it! Tanner sagged back further on his couch, reaching up to press both palms against his closed eyelids with a sigh. Having that sort of control, that kind of knockout seduction, ought to be illegal, he considered. When she pulled him to her, drew his lips to her chest, ran her fingernails along the length of his spine while pressing just deep enough to leave little furrows in his skin-

He needed to stop thinking about this. Tanner went to the custom bar that he'd had installed in a corner of his living room, poured himself a slug of generic whiskey. No point in breaking out the good stuff, not so late at night.

He tossed back the slug in a single gulp. He barely felt the fire as it went down his throat and settled into his stomach. He doled out another two fingers of amber liquid, dropped back down on the couch, stared down into the glass.

This was a good thing, he tried to tell himself. He could use this. If Alicia was willing to sleep with him, she truly believed in this truce. He could make use of that belief, turn it to his advantage in order to ferret out the information he needed. This was a sign that Senator Stone trusted him, in the office as well as in the confines of her apartment.

All he had to do was think logically about this, keep himself distanced and not let his emotions get in the way.

Hell, he went on, attempting to console himself. This didn't even mean that he needed to stop sleeping with the woman - far from it! The more he fucked her, the more she'd come to trust him, the more certain she'd be that he believed in this truce as much as she did. He'd earn her trust, learn all her weaknesses, and then strike at just the right moment to bring this bill crashing down in flames.

But could he separate himself from his feelings, detach his mind from the emotions? Even sitting here, with his eyes closed, all he saw was the lines of Alicia Stone's naked, perfect body, soft and warm and reaching out to draw him in and envelop him with her embrace...

Tanner grunted, slammed the glass of whiskey down onto his coffee table. Bed, he thought distantly to himself. He needed to go to bed, get some sleep. It was far too late - he'd already stayed out longer than he intended at the restaurant with Alicia, and then adding on the time for what happened afterward-

-soft, warmth, her wet mouth pressed against his, her body arching towards him and crying out for more, that soft little moan from the back of her throat whenever he drove himself all the way inside of her to fill her with his power, how eagerly she clutched at him, refusing to let him take it easy, needing him to take her with everything, make her come, make her scream in pleasure at the top of her lungs-

In his bedroom, Tanner flopped down face first onto his massive mattress, not even bothering to extract himself from his clothes. They were quite soiled already, after spending time scattered about Alicia's room. He'd have to send the whole suit off to the dry cleaner's; the thing stank of sex.

Grabbing a pillow, Tanner pulled it up, over his face. Even now, dammit, he couldn't get her out of his mind! Just lying in the sheets, the pillow blocking the bedroom light from his eyes, he could practically feel her next to him, could remember how warm and soft her body felt as it pressed against his own. Despite the punishment it had received, his cock flexed once again in his pants, as if hopeful that there might be yet another round in store.

Was this all because he'd taken time off from his usual hunt for women in bars and at clubs? It couldn't be. He'd gone for long breaks of time without having a woman before, and he hadn't fallen for the first young lady to break his dry spell. Sure, he could close his eyes and think back to a litany of healthy, flushed, nubile bodies that joined him in his bed (or in an alley, a bathroom stall, against a wall, on a couch, even in the middle of a swimming pool on one especially memorable night), but he'd never felt this rush of pure, overwhelming need towards any of those women before.

What made Alicia Stone any different?

Calm. Deep breaths. Think about something, anything else. Tanner struggled upright once again, forced himself to take off the soiled clothing. He hung the suit on a hanger, made a mental note to himself to drop it at the dry cleaner's.

Now what? He crawled back into his bed, beneath the sheets, but he knew that he wouldn't be able to sleep. After a moment, he grunted and sat back up, padding in bare feet back out into his apartment.

He headed over to the second bedroom, one which Tanner had converted into his own private gym. He settled down on the bench, his bare back pressed against the fabric, looking up at the loaded bar on the rack above him. Pulling in a deep breath, he gripped the bar and lifted it up, forcing his way through a set of bench presses.

The bar clanged loudly as he dropped it back onto the rack's hooks, and Tanner breathed deeply for a moment as he savored the burn in his pectoral muscles. He sat up, looking around the room.

Curls next. He crossed to the rack of dumbbells, picked up a pair of forty-pounders. It felt good to lift them up, feeling the bulging muscle of his bicep sliding back and forth across his upper arm with each flex. He pumped through a set, then carefully lowered the dumbbells down to the ground. He had installed a thick mat in case he dropped any weights, but didn't want to risk accidentally crushing one of his toes.

Slowly, methodically, Tanner worked out each of his major muscle groups, moving in a slow circuit around the room. He pushed himself through five full sets, a complete workout, despite the fact that he had now stayed up well past midnight. The clock mounted on the wall above the door read nearly three AM by the time he re-racked his weights.

Tanner looked down at his body, now gleaming with sweat. His mind felt more relaxed, now, the physical effort of exercise also consuming some of the manic mental energy that had kept him from falling asleep. Not bothering to even duck into the shower, he grabbed a towel, gave himself a quick rubdown, and then dropped into bed.

This time, when he closed his eyes, he felt sleep already hovering just beyond his reach. As he settled deeper into his mattress, it came in, reaching out with silent fingers to carry him away into unconsciousness.

But still, even as he drifted further down, away from wakefulness, Tanner couldn't help but replay the events of that night. Where had he slipped up? Where, exactly, did the night go off book, slip away from his plan?

It happened, he decided, from the moment that he first arrived at Bayou, only to find that Alicia had already beaten him there and was sitting at the table.

More than that, even - she'd already had time to order - and receive - a drink! Seeing her sitting there in the booth, his booth, his favorite spot, looking calm and composed with that drink in her hand, Tanner had been off balance. He'd never quite managed to recover from that point.

Taking advantage of his little stumble, Alicia had brought up the idea of a truce - and he, seeing no other option, accepted.

What might he have done differently? If he'd not taken the truce, he might never have gotten Alicia to open up to him, reveal more of her plan - but Tanner had faced aggressive opponents before and triumphed. He'd crushed bills without needing to cozy up to their sponsors. He could have denied the truce, cut all ties with Alicia, and still found a way to crush her bill before it ever made it to the floor of the Senate for a vote.

But at the time, it seemed to him like his only option was to accept that truce. He'd accepted, and thus slipped further into Alicia's sphere of influence.

So what next?

Sleepy, comfortable, but still not quite ready to relinquish his last little grip on consciousness, Tanner thought ahead to the next few days. He really did want to get into bed with Alicia again - he couldn't deny that truth. But there certainly had to be a way for him to accomplish both his goals - sleep with Alicia, and still bring down her education bill.

All he had to do was wait for the right opportunity to present itself, and make sure to take it. No hesitation. When that opportunity arrived, he'd strike like a cobra. It would likely be the end of the relationship between them, but he could surely survive that small loss. He'd sleep with the senator a few more times, get tired of her, and move on, just like he'd always done in the past.

But for now, he only needed to watch, and wait, and keep his eyes open. He'd continue to go along with this truce, play the straight man. He'd keep on sleeping with Alicia, let her convince herself that she was seeing his true personality. She'd believe that, given how he supported her, he truly believed in her side, at least for the next two weeks.

Besides, Tanner added, smiling a little to himself in the darkness. Two weeks of sex with a powerful U.S. Senator, one who was definitely the most attractive woman in Congress? Who would turn down that opportunity? Hell, Freddie would probably burst a blood vessel when Tanner told him about this new development.

Yes, he had things under control. All he had to do was, in the back of his mind, keep his true intentions clear. He could have his fun, enjoy himself - and then, when the time came, he'd do the right thing.

He'd do his job.

With that, Tanner finally drifted away, borne into blackness on the wings of sleep.

CHAPTER FOURTEEN

Over the next few days, Tanner found himself grappling with a surprising emotion, one that, for a while, he couldn't even find the right words to describe.

"Love," Freddie said, almost a week later, as they sipped at beers in the Capitol Lounge together. "Is that why it's been so hard for me to get ahold of you? You don't return my calls, man."

"I don't return most calls, even those from people much higher than you on the food chain," Tanner replied automatically, and then shook his head. "No, it's not love. I don't fall in love."

"Uh huh." Tanner saw Freddie roll his eyes, not even trying to hide the expression. "Come on, man, you can't stop thinking about her, you need her even after already getting her in bed, the sex is amazing, she's like no other woman that you've ever known - sounds a lot like love to me."

Tanner sighed, shook his head and took another gulp of beer. It didn't hold a candle to the complexity of a great scotch or bourbon, but he wanted to not get too out of control tonight. "Anyway, I've been working like a dog on this latest project, so I'm sorry that I haven't gotten to call you back."

"Apology accepted," Freddie said. "And what is this new project, anyway? You've been pretty hush-hush with the details so far."

"Secrecy here, okay? No telling anyone." Tanner had trusted his friend with the details of some of his assignments before, but he turned to Freddie, narrowing his eyes to underscore the importance of this instruction.

Freddie held up one hand, extending two fingers in a vague approximation of the scout's sign. "Promise. Lips are sealed."

Tanner knew that Freddie meant his words. "Okay. The politician that I'm working with is the new freshman Senator, Alicia Stone. She's planning on bringing this big education bill to the floor, and she's doing her damndest to drill up support for it and ensure that it will pass." He paused for a moment to take a sip of his beer. "And I need to kill it."

After a second of letting this sink in, he saw his buddy's eyes widen. "Wait a minute," Freddie sputtered. "You're lying to this woman and pretending to help her with her bill, while secretly scheming to kill it. And meanwhile, at the same time, you're sleeping with her, and really falling for her!? Are you crazy?"

"I'm not falling for her," Tanner corrected, but Freddie was too far past this point to be stopped.

"Holy shit, man. That's beyond the pale. That's totally insane. You're falling for the girl that you're going to betray - and she's a damn Senator!" Freddie gaped at Tanner, his eyes wide as his mouth hung open. "How the hell do you get into crazy situations like this?"

"I'm not falling-" Tanner decided to not even bother finishing that sentence; it didn't seem to be sinking into Freddie's head, anyway. Instead, he just moved forward.

"You're not giving me much in the way of advice."

"Advice?" Freddie choked out, nearly coughing up half his beer. "I mean, this is so outside of my realm of experience, it's not even funny! This is like hopping into a time machine, going back a thousand years, and asking a tribesman how to install the latest version of Windows on your laptop! This is like going to a hermit living at the north pole and asking them for the best way to grill up a jaguar steak! This is like, like, like hitting on the wife of the President himself!"

"Actually, I met her one time, and she cast a pretty randy eye on me," Tanner volunteered, making Freddie collapse into a fit of uncontrollable coughing.

"Anyway," he gasped out, when he finally cleared his throat. "What have the two of you been doing together?"

"During the day, or in the evenings?"

Tanner watched as Freddie hesitated, not sure whether he wanted to hear about the high-level work in the Capitol, or if he wanted to indulge his vicarious side by hearing about Tanner's nighttime exploits. "Start with the days," he said finally.

Before answering, Tanner downed the last of his beer, setting it down on the bartop with a clink. The bartender, a dark-haired Asian with a gravity-defying set of tits, sashayed over with a smile to bring Tanner a refill, but he scarcely even noticed. He didn't even spare a glance for the woman! Inside his head, a little part of him wondered if he had something seriously wrong. Maybe he'd developed a brain tumor, altering his behavior...

"Let's see," he began. "With a big bill like this, asking for potentially billions of dollars to be diverted, you can't just toss it out during a session. This needs multiple sponsors, and ideally, you want to know that you've secured enough agreements from other senators to guarantee the bill's passage, before it ever reaches the floor of the Senate. Even better is to have a good margin of error; there's always the chance that a couple of your supporters will end up flip-flopping and voting against it, for a variety of reasons."

"Sometimes, it's because you get to them," Freddie filled in, and Tanner nodded.

"Yes. Sometimes. But in any case, we've been dashing around from office to office, trying to drum up support for the bill. On one hand, it's education, and it's very tough to find someone who will publicly state that they'll vote against funding more American education. This bill could reduce student debts and simultaneously make our young adults more competitive with those from other countries; that's a powerful lure."

"So why would anyone vote against it?"

"Oh, there's a million reasons. Fiscal responsibility, concern about budgets, how the money will be spent, and of course there's the constant fight over pork barrel spending." Tanner saw Freddie's brow furrow, and explained. "Every senator wants to add his own little project to the bill, something for his home state, his constituents. That's usually extra, outside the scope of the bill - it's pork, alongside the meat of the bill itself. But each thing that's added further inflates the bill's total cost, and no one wants to see that another senator is getting a pork project while they aren't getting one for their own home state. It's a constant battle, trying to appease everyone without compromising too far."

"Ah, got it. And that's how bills end up costing five times as much as they were supposed to, originally, right?" Freddie asked.

"That's right," Tanner nodded. "And trying to balance everything, predict how ninety-nine other people are going to end up voting, is exhausting. So we're spending most of our days working on that. We've got this huge board with a list of all the senators in each camp - for, against, and on the fence - and we're constantly scrawling new information on the board or dragging individuals from one camp to another."

"Okay," Freddie said after digesting this for a minute. "So what about outside of work?"

Tanner sighed. He couldn't help it; Alicia really did have a hold on his brain! "It's driving me crazy! This damn woman is like a drug, Freddie! I keep on seeing her every night; when I try to take a night off, it just feels empty, somehow! We've gone out to movies, visited restaurants - but all we really want to do is get back to her place, or sometimes mine, and rip off each other's clothes and go crazy!"

Taking a deep breath, he reached up and ran a hand through his hair. "I always tell myself that I'll resist, that I've got control over myself. And then all I have to do is catch a glimpse of her, have her crook her finger and beckon me, and I go running over like a damn dog!"

Freddie made a noncommittal sound in his throat, but Tanner just kept on plunging forward. "And what's worst of all is that I used to be totally fine on my own, doing something like hitting a bar or club, or hanging out with you and grabbing a drink. But even now, I keep on thinking about her, wondering what she's doing! I want to text her, even right now!"

He turned to Freddie, his eyes wide. He needed advice, help. At the beginning of the week, Tanner had been certain that he could stay on top of his feelings.

Now, he wasn't so sure.

Freddie just looked steadily back at him. "You know, I'm not sure that I see the problem here," he commented.

"You don't see the problem?" Tanner repeated in shock. "Freddie, this woman is turning my entire damn life upside down! My whole career is built on not being tied to anyone, being able to do whatever's necessary! And now I can't even focus, because I keep on thinking about how much I want to tear her clothes off and take her against the nearest solid surface!"

"Maybe it's time for a new career. You've been working as a fixer for a while now, haven't you?"

Tanner sighed in exasperation. This talk with Freddie definitely wasn't turning out like he'd hoped. "Yes, but I've built it into my career. This isn't just some job where I can drop it and step right into another field. I've made a name for myself, and I've got all my connections, all my history - if I walk away, that's all worthless!"

"So." Freddie downed the last of his own beer, looked around for the bartender. Somehow, he doubted that he'd get the same level of service as Tanner received. That was alright, however; he had Cristina's phone number burning a hole in his cell phone. After their first date last week, he'd seen her again, had quite a nice time with her. After she moved past her initial shyness, she proved quite witty, delightful for conversations as well as a lovely handful in bed.

"So what?"

"So it looks like you're currently torn between job and romance," he pointed out. "You can't have both. Time to make a choice."

"Well, it's an easy choice, isn't it?" Tanner answered. He lapsed off into silence as Freddie waited.

"And the easy choice is…"

"Career, obviously." Tanner snorted, as if this answer ought to have been obvious. Freddie clearly didn't understand the importance, the value, of his job. No one else could do what he did.

"Right. Of course." Freddie shrugged. "So you've made the choice. What's the problem with it?"

"No problem," Tanner said. "No problem at all."

And that should be the end of it, he thought to himself. He valued his career far more than whatever he could call the strange and unclear situation between himself and Senator Alicia Stone. Sure, he had some sort of strange attraction to her for now, but it would surely fade after time. He'd get past her. And his career would continue; he'd maintain his support as the top fixer for the RNC.

He just had to keep on telling himself that he didn't need Alicia. He was fully happy before she entered his life. He'd be happy without her, after she was gone.

But then again, he didn't need to worry about that for now. He could relax, enjoy his time with Alicia. Freddie did have a point - he'd always have his career, even after this thing with the woman, whatever it was, ran its course.

But he could take in the moment, have a good time with Alicia.

Maybe he did need to rethink his pickup game, start looking for more of a relationship, even after this ended, he considered to himself. Not with Alicia, of course. Not with a Democrat, a politician, someone who saw through all his illusions. Someone in the Republican background noise, not in the spotlight, someone more suitable for him.

But that could come later.

For now, he could enjoy Alicia. Especially her body, that way her ass curved when she reclined on her bed or the couch and read through a bill or white paper, those sardonic, taunting looks she sent his way to tell that she saw right through his bullshit, but wanted him anyway, the little moan that always escaped her lips when he ran his fingers over her, teasing her with what he would do, but only when she begged him for it…

Yes, Tanner told himself. Things were good now. No need to worry about rushing too quickly to what the future would change.

Of course, as he left the Capitol Lounge that evening to grab a ride back to his penthouse apartment, he didn't know that a crossroads lurked in his future. The bill's vote was another week away, and there was still a decision to be made:

Betray Alicia, or betray the Republicans, the side he'd

worked to support all his life.

Tanner, a man who never shirked from anything in his life, found himself procrastinating on making this decision.

CHAPTER FIFTEEN

"Oh my gawd, Alicia! This is crazy! We're in, like, Washington!"

Alicia held back her wince as Jamie, an old friend from her college days back in Colorado, looked around with excitement after issuing this statement, speaking perhaps a little too loudly. Jamie had always been the life of the party back at university, and it seemed like her ebullient, energetic personality hadn't diminished in the years since then.

"You get used to it quickly," she offered, taking a sip from her glass of wine. "After a while, it just feels like another city, like all the rest."

Jamie, however, shook her head. "No way, girl. This is so cool - you're representing our entire state-"

"Half of the state-"

"-and making real laws and stuff! This is so cool!" She looked around, as if expecting the President himself to come striding into the wine bar and ask for a glass of Pinot Grigio. "Any chance that you can try and lower my taxes?"

When Alicia picked up her phone earlier that afternoon and saw Jamie's number calling her, she almost didn't answer. What in the world could the other woman want? As it turned out, however, Jamie had been in town for an unrelated matter and decided to look up her old college friend. Tanner had already informed Alicia that he was grabbing a drink tonight with some friend of his, so she figured that it might be nice to catch up and reminisce about old times.

"Unfortunately, my job doesn't quite work like that," she answered Jamie. "But how's life going? I haven't heard much from you since college. What are you up to?"

"Oh my gawd, Alicia! Like, so much!" With a big grin, Jamie burst into a long spiel about how she'd headed off to work for some pharmaceutical company as a sales rep, and ended up getting really great numbers and winning a free vacation, paid for by the company. "And I get to go and meet all these cute doctors, and oh, they're so adorable! I swear, I've fallen in love at least a dozen times since I started this job. Did you ever watch Grey's Anatomy, Alicia? You know McDreamy?"

"Actually, I don't have a lot of time for television-"

"Well, I swear, every third doctor is, like, that attractive. Like, they should be prescribing me some sort of meds, because I get hot flashes when I'm around them!" Beaming, Jamie theatrically fanned herself, and then paused to take another gulp of her own wine. "But actually, there's this one guy, and he's asked me out, like, six times already, so I finally broke down and decided to say yes…"

Sitting back, Alicia let Jamie's flood of words wash comfortably over her. Jamie had the amazing ability to make little tiny issues in her life, the kind of things that no one else would consider for more than a second, into world-breaking concerns. In a way, it was rather comforting to listen to her. Knowing that someone like Jamie thought this much about whether or not to wear a pink blouse with purple capri pants made Alicia feel a little better about her own decisions.

"...and so, since it was our third date and everything, I finally let him take me back to his house, and you won't believe what he's got there!" Jamie paused, her eyes sparkling, and Alicia suddenly realized that the other woman was waiting for her input.

"Um, a wine cellar?"

"Wouldn't that be amazing?" Jamie sighed, stretching out the word 'amazing' to at least four syllables. "But no, it's almost as good - he had a hot tub! And I don't want to spill, but we kind of went in. Even though I didn't think to bring a bathing suit on the date!" She giggled and pretended to look away demurely, even as her tone practically begged Alicia to ask for all the sultry details.

Alicia was silent for a beat too long, and Jamie sighed. "So what have you been up to since college? Anything fun?" she asked, even as her eyes roamed around the room, perhaps searching for her next McDreamy, whatever that was.

"Well, I'm a US Senator," Alicia pointed out dryly. "That's recent, and it is pretty engaging-"

"Oh, not that. Come on, you know what I mean! Boys!" Jamie frowned. "Even back in college, you were always the quiet one, with your nose buried in a book. You never went out to any of the fun parties. I always felt bad, worried you were missing out."

"I had boyfriends, at least!" Alicia replied, wondering why she was trying to defend herself.

"Sure, but they always came second to all those textbooks. What about now? Are you seeing anyone?"

Alicia paused, trying to decide whether to mention Tanner. The pause was a mistake, however, and Jamie pounced. "Aha! I knew it, you are! Come on, you need to tell me everything! I promise that I won't leak any secrets to the press, I'm not that kind of girl to kiss and tell!"

Hah. Jamie was exactly the kind of girl who would kiss and tell - but on the other hand, Alicia knew that she had absolutely zero interest in politics. She couldn't even name the difference between a Republican and a Democrat, much less see the issues with their contrasting ideologies. On a whim, Alicia decided that she needed to tell someone, and Jamie might be the best person to choose.

"Okay, fine, there's a guy," she broke down, and Jamie practically fell off her seat with excitement. "But it's really new, only been going on for a couple of weeks. I don't know much about where it's going-"

"Phooey, the first couple of weeks are the best part!" Jamie insisted. "Trust me, I usually just focus on the first couple weeks. So what's he like?"

"What's he like?" Alicia paused, considering. "Well, he's tall."

"A good start," Jamie murmured, leaning in as if craning to catch every single detail.

"And he's got a hell of a body - he's like a god of the gym." Despite herself, Alicia found herself really getting into talking about Tanner. "And I don't want to kiss and tell-"

"Do, do!"

"-but he knows what he's doing in bed, too." She sighed, smiling as she remembered their most recent date, how they spent most of the evening just fighting against their urges to rush home and rip off each other's clothes. "God, if I'd met a guy like him in college, I definitely would not have gotten nearly as good grades!"

"Yeah, girl! Get it!" Jamie raised her wine glass, and Alicia enthusiastically clinked her own against it. "And it's new, I get it, but do you think it's going somewhere?"

The smile slipped a little on Alicia's face. Honestly, she'd been trying not to think about the future with Tanner. It was still uncertain, to be sure, but it wasn't looking incredibly promising.

After all, they did have the end of the truce, coming up in under a week. The bill was going to be called to a vote, and then the truce would end. Would Tanner immediately turn around and go back to trying to sabotage her, make some attempt to stab her in the back? Would he expect her to keep on sleeping with him, even as, professionally, they did their best to destroy each other?

Somehow, Alicia couldn't see that working out as a viable dating strategy.

But maybe he'd be willing to consider making a different choice, something that could let them continue to see each other. They hadn't discussed it - most of their dates, they barely managed to do anything more than catch up a little on each other's days before they dove into bed and ripped off each other's clothes, putting their mouths and energy to better uses. Still, Alicia saw the way that Tanner looked at her, even after they'd both finished and as they both lay in each other's arms and waited for their breathing to return to normal. That was the look of more than just simple lust.

Maybe, just maybe, they could find some way to make a future together.

Alicia realized that Jamie was still looking at her, still expecting an answer. "I think it's too early to say, one way or another," she remarked, lightly shrugging off the topic. "But for now, I'm enjoying things at where they are."

"Hey, that sounds totally good with me," Jamie said, lifting her hands (which, coincidentally, also brought the wine glass up to her lips). "I mean, I'm not one to lecture anybody on their dating habits! But it's good to see that you're actually seeing someone. I can tell, you know."

"You can?" Alicia asked, surprised.

"Oh, sure. You're practically glowing, girl! And you haven't even looked one time at that really cute bartender who's been throwing flirty looks at our table all night."

Now, Alicia did glance over at the bartender in question. Definitely not her type - too skinny, with sleeve tattoos on his exposed arms. He caught her looking over at him, and he raised a suggestive eyebrow, giving her a rakish grin.

She quickly pulled her eyes away. Definitely not.

"Well, I won't push you any further - although I can tell you that I'm still totally curious about this mystery guy of yours," Jamie said, after finishing off her glass of wine. "You don't have any pictures of him, do you?"

"Actually, I've got a couple." Alicia drew out her phone and showed Jamie, who whistled in appreciation when she saw them.

"Damn! And you've got him! Girl, you need to, like, tell me all your secrets!"

Easy - just see through his bullshit and second-guess everything he says and does, Alicia thought privately to herself. This, however, was not the time to say any of that out loud. So instead, she shrugged and did her best to look demure. "Work more? That's where I meet him."

"Well, I do meet lots of doctors at work, it's true," Jamie nodded. "But honestly, it's just so much more fun to go out on three dollar margarita night, find a cutie, and grind up on him until he gets the idea!"

The image of Jamie out in some bar, a margarita in one hand and her butt pressed firmly against the crotch of some poor, unsuspecting man made Alicia laugh. "It's good of you to come out and see me, Jamie."

"Hey, I'm on vacation! And even back in college, we all knew that you were going to do great. Remember when we helped make campaign posters so you could run for the student council, or something?"

"Executive Student Board of the college. And I lost that election, remember?"

"Yeah, but only because the girl who won had posted a topless video on her public Facebook page and everyone shared it around." Jamie cast an eye at Alicia's outfit, considering. "Although if you do ever need a boost in the re-election polls, you could always take a note out of her book…"

"Hah. Not happening, not funny." Alicia crossed her arms across her chest, imagining the damage that a leak of some sort of inappropriate pictures would do to her reputation - and her re-election chances.

"Just throwing it out there." Jamie nodded towards Alicia's glass, still with an ounce or so of wine left in it. "Now here, finish that off! I want to get another glass, but if I go up there without you, I'll totally just come off as a lush. And when you shoot down that poor bartender, he'll probably be super happy that I'm interested!"

"So I'm playing wingman to you," Alicia theatrically groaned, but she gulped down the last of her wine and headed up to the bar with her friend. Briefly, she wondered if Tanner was doing all right, if he was thinking about her. She almost drew out her phone to text him, but forced herself to let it be.

What the two of them had together was new, still in its infancy - but if things kept going as they were, didn't change, they might actually have a shot at success together.

CHAPTER SIXTEEN

"So, this is it," Tanner said, surprised to hear the nervousness in his own voice. "What do you think?"

He watched as Alicia entered his penthouse, slowly turned around, taking it in. Her eyes roamed over the bookshelves, the leather sofa and armchairs, the expensive Tiffany lamps and the marble gas fireplace installed against one wall. Finally, they returned back to his own, and he caught that dangerous little glint in them.

"I like it," she said, but Tanner didn't yet release his breath. "You'll have to pass on my congratulations to whatever designer from Restoration Hardware actually put the place together."

There's the stinger, Tanner thought to himself. "Why, what do you mean?" he asked aloud, trying to affect an air of injured innocence.

She just pointed back at him. "Don't play that card with me. It's nice, Tanner, but it's just so... sterile."

"Sterile?" He frowned, looking around at the opulent furnishings, the perfect combination of wealth and good taste. "What's sterile about it?"

"I mean, every single thing in here looks pretty much perfect. But if you slapped price tags on them, you'd have a hard time convincing me that I wasn't in a showroom at some furniture store!" Alicia sat down on the leather couch, and Tanner swallowed as he thought about how perfect she looked, lounging there. "Where's the Keegan Tanner personal touch?"

He shrugged. "Maybe I just don't feel the need to make all of my decorations personal."

But as he took a seat on the couch beside Alicia, she kept scrutinizing him, making him feel a little like a bug trapped under a microscope. "What?" he asked, finally.

"You know, Keegan, I don't know much about you," Alicia commented.

"Keegan?" he answered, grimacing. "Come on, I hate being called by my first name."

"I've noticed. Do you think that it's a defense mechanism, a way to shield yourself from anyone prying into your history, by using just your last name?"

He shrugged. "I just like the sound of my last name better, I guess."

Alicia just kept on watching him. "You asked me a lot of personal questions on the night that we agreed to our truce," she said.

"You mean the night that we first kissed, hooked up?" Tanner replied, trying to inject a little humor, but Alicia just nodded, her eyes still locked on him. "So?"

"So whenever I asked one, you kind of dodged it," she answered. "If I ask some now, are you going to do that again?"

Tanner sighed, but it seemed like Alicia wasn't going to let this conversational topic go. "Fine. Take your best shot, and I'll try and answer."

She smiled, sitting back and tapping her chin with a finger. "Here, how about we make this interesting?"

"How so?"

Her smile grew wider. "Each time you answer a question of mine with a serious, in-depth answer, I'll take off an article of clothing."

That caught Tanner's attention. "Hah, deal."

"Great." She paused and considered her first question. "How often do you talk to your parents?"

That wasn't the question that Tanner expected, and he dropped back a little on the couch. "Am I allowed to pass on a question?"

Alicia's flat look was all the answer that he needed. "Fine. If I had to approximate... I'd say about never."

"Really? Why not?"

"Hey, I answered your question," he pointed out, nodding towards her shirt, but she shook her head, hair swinging back and forth across her shoulders.

"Doesn't count as a full answer. You need to explain why."

"I feel like you're adding additional rules," he complained, but kept talking. "Fine. My dad left when I was a baby, so I don't know where he is, or really anything about him. My mom wasn't thrilled with my decision to go into politics, let's just say that." His mouth twisted sourly. "Ironic, that is."

"Why's it ironic?"

He didn't even bother to point out that she'd asked another question. "Because I first went into this job to get enough money to pay for her retirement home. She doesn't have dementia, not exactly, but she gets angry and bitter, thinks that life's just out to get her. She can't go out and do much on her own, so I paid for her home."

"That's kind of you," Alicia said, but Tanner shook his head, suddenly angry. He grabbed a pillow, squeezing it as if he could strangle his mother by proxy.

"No, it's selfish of me. She kept on nagging me, insisting that I was doing everything wrong, but never offering any suggestions that would help me. There's nothing like knowing that nothing you can do is ever going to be good enough, that you're just a failure in her eyes, like everything else in the world."

He squeezed his eyes shut. "Like my father was."

A moment later, Tanner felt Alicia's soft hand press against his cheek. "I'm sorry," she murmured, her big eyes holding his, soft and caring. "I didn't know - we don't have to keep on talking about this-"

"No, I might as well get it out," Tanner said after taking a deep breath. "But yeah, parents aren't really in the picture."

"Got it." Alicia considered for a minute, as Tanner forced his white-knuckled fingers to let go of the pillow. "What about brothers? Sisters?"

"Nope. Apparently, I was enough. More than enough, if you ever listened to my mother." Tanner looked up at Alicia. "I don't remember asking you about this. Do you have siblings?"

"An older sister, but she's dropped off the grid," Alicia said with a shrug. "She was a bit of a wild child, while I was the goody two-shoes. She's off in India, last time I checked in with her, doing some sort of project where she builds houses for some of the villages hit by the latest tsunami, or something like that."

"Sounds very noble," Tanner noted, which made Alicia snort.

"Not at all. She just doesn't want to face real life, have to ever consider having a husband, or kids, or a house, or even a permanent address. So she keeps on throwing herself into these charity missions instead."

Alicia drifted off, looking off into space as if remembering her sister, but then pulled her eyes back to Tanner. "Anyway, next question. What do you want in the future?"

"What do you mean?"

She spread her hands out. "I mean, what do you see

your future as like? Are you just going to keep working as a fixer, probably dragging random women home from some club who are half your age, until you drop dead of a heart attack? What's your long term goal?"

Tanner opened his mouth to reply, but paused. "I guess I haven't really thought about one," he finally answered. "I suppose that, someday, I wouldn't mind having kids."

"Really?" Alicia asked, raising her eyebrows.

"Don't get any ideas," he shot back, pointing a warning finger at her. "But maybe in the future. It would be nice to prove to myself that I can be a better parent than my mom was."

"You aren't worried that you might make mistakes?"

"What, me? When have I ever made a mistake?" Tanner asked, puffing up his chest pompously. Alicia laughed and reached across the couch to smack him, and he smiled back at her. "Hell, I'll probably make a lot of mistakes. But I'll learn from them, and keep trying. In the end, I think i'll do a pretty good job. At least by the third or fourth kid, I'll probably have it down."

For a moment, they both sat silently, gazing off into the future. Finally, Alicia cleared her throat.

"One last question," she said.

Tanner sighed, rolled his eyes, but nodded. "Fine. Shoot."

Alicia paused for a few seconds, and Tanner watched as she unconsciously did this cute little expression where she furrowed her brow and pursed her lips. They moved slightly, as if she was trying out different combinations of questions inside her head before voicing any of them out loud. For some reason, Tanner found the gesture to be cute but also intimate, as if he was catching a little glimpse into her head.

"Okay," she finally said, returning her attention back to Tanner. "If you could go back and change one thing in your past, what would you pick?"

He didn't know how to respond. "Um, give me a minute," he said weakly after a few seconds, trying to think. Alicia just nodded, waiting on him as he tried to think back.

If he could go back and change something in his past? He tried to imagine what would have the biggest positive impact on his life. He could make his dad stay around, maybe have a complete family. He could have chosen to go talk to the Democrats, not the Republicans, when he first went looking for a job, maybe ended up in a job where he did more for the future besides holding it back, where he didn't have to face the conflict of whether he'd choose to betray this amazing woman that he found himself really liking, or give up on his career…

"Okay, I've got something," he finally said.

"I'm all ears." And indeed, Alicia leaned in, her eyes drinking him in, glued to his words and waiting for his answer.

"Back in high school, there was this cute girl - head cheerleader, blonde, really pretty. She always smiled at me, but I didn't have the confidence that I possess now." He tried a smirk, but it fell flat. "I always thought that she liked me, for some reason that I couldn't guess, but I never did anything about it."

"And?" Alicia asked, after he paused for a minute.

Tanner sighed. "If I could change something, I'd go back and ask her out. Just go for it, even though she'd likely shoot me down."

After a second, Alicia sat back, frowning a little at him as she crossed her arms across her chest. "Maybe not the answer that I expected," she commented, narrowing her eyes at him.

"It's not just because she was cute," Tanner countered. He sighed. "It was after the end of that grade, in fact, that I realized that nothing was going to change for me unless I went out and did it for myself. Somehow, I'd imagined that the girl would see me for who I was, and she'd want to go out with me because of it."

"But it didn't happen."

"No. And I learned that it's not what I happen to believe on the inside, but what I project on the outside that truly matters." Tanner sighed. "A hard lesson, but it's served me well ever since that day. But sometimes, I wonder what might have happened if I didn't chicken out, if I didn't let myself grow jaded and cynical."

Across the couch from him, Alicia loosened her hands from where she'd crossed them, leaning forward to rest one gently on Tanner's knee. He felt the heat of her touch, and even her gentle contact made him hyper-aware of her presence, the faint floral, clean scent of her in the air.

"Keegan," she murmured, and Tanner looked up at the unexpected use of his name.

Before he could ask what she wanted, however, she leaned in and kissed him.

This wasn't a kiss of passion, he realized immediately with the small part of his brain that wasn't busy shooting off fireworks. This was soft and gentle, barely brushing against his lips, delicate as a butterfly's wings. He wrapped his arms around her with tenderness, almost afraid that she might break.

But she didn't, and her kiss deepened, her lips pushing in against his, opening slightly, inviting him inside.

"I should head home," she whispered to him, not pulling away.

"Probably," he answered, holding onto her, never wanting to let her go. This woman, who had just heard his deepest secret, who still offered herself up to him, who still smiled at him from where she sat in his lap. "Lots to do in the next couple of days. Bill's almost here."

Truce is almost up. He didn't say it, didn't want to think about it.

"I should leave," Alicia repeated again, but still didn't

make a move away from his arms.

"Well?" he finally asked.

Her smile deepened, those enchanting eyes starting to spark. "Convince me to stay."

Surprisingly, Tanner didn't have to try as hard as he expected to succeed.

CHAPTER SEVENTEEN

"Tanner, get your ass in here!"

Rubbing his eyes as he sipped his espresso, Tanner hit the "delete" button on his answering machine. He'd received enough calls from Richard Pribus, head of the Republican National Committee, to gauge the man's moods based on his tone.

And in this particular voicemail, Pribus was hitting at least an eight, possibly a nine, on a ten-point scale of his anger.

Alicia had already left, rolling out of bed at an ungodly early hour, insisting that she needed to get going. "I still have my morning run, and I need to hit at least three other offices before lunch," she said, searching around on the floor to try and find where her underwear landed. "Listen, have you seen my panties?"

"Nope," Tanner sleepily replied, clutching the stolen undergarment tightly in his hand, hidden under the pillow.

"Oh well." Alicia gave him a bawdily naughty wink as she leaned in to kiss him goodbye. "Hopefully, you won't be distracted all day as you think of me going commando."

FIXER

Her revenge worked; Tanner immediately felt himself grow hard, and he tried to reach out to pull her back in bed-

-only for Alicia to snatch back her panties from his outstretched hand. "Talk to you later!" she told him, bouncing out of his apartment.

With a groan, Tanner flopped back over, not getting up until he couldn't bear to listen to the repetitive beep of his answering machine any longer. But as soon as he heard the message from Pribus, he rushed to get dressed.

"Morning, Mr. Tanner," Charlie the security guard called out as Tanner headed quickly through the lobby of the RNC's building. "In a hurry?"

Tanner might be running slightly late - DC traffic this morning proved even more snarled and tangled than usual - but he still managed to give the elderly guard a smile and a nod. "And Pribus has a stick up his ass about something. Apparently I'm the one with answers."

Charlie just shook his head. "You need to be careful, you know that?" he admonished. "That man's a petty tyrant, no offense to him as my boss's boss's boss, and he works you too hard. You need to think about yourself, too."

The man's words made a little shiver run down Tanner's back, their content echoing some of Freddie's remarks from the night before. "Thanks, Charlie, I'll keep it in mind," he said, as the elevator dinged to announce its arrival. "See you later."

Up outside of Pribus's office, Tanner didn't have time to flirt with the man's receptionist. As soon as he stepped out of the elevator, Pribus spotted him, snapping his fingers angrily at Tanner as he stalked into his office. Tanner quickly followed after the head of the RNC.

"Well?" Pribus demanded as soon as Tanner cleared the threshold of his office, not even giving him time to close the door and grant them some privacy.

Tanner took a deep breath as he closed the door.

Pribus was well known for his mercurial moods, swinging from positive to stormy in an instant. "Well, what?"

He received a huff of air in response. "Well, how's the weather outside? The education bill, of course! Is this thing dead in the water yet?"

"I'm... I'm working on it," Tanner tried, watching as Pribus stomped around to sit down heavily in the chair behind his desk.

"Working on it," Pribus repeated. He didn't sound satisfied.

Tanner spread his hands open. "Look, this is complex. it's not like just walking in and throwing the book at Alicia for doing something wrong-"

"Yes, that's exactly how it should be!" Pribus interrupted. "Tanner, you've got no idea how much heat is coming down my neck over this damn bill. Apparently, this infernal bitch of a senator has been setting up meetings with everyone and their uncle, on both sides of the aisle!" His eyes narrowed at Tanner. "And word is that you're sitting in on most of these meetings, too. What's going on? You thinking of jumping ship?"

"Of course not!" Tanner replied automatically. He'd taken a seat in the chair across from Pribus's desk, but he now leaned forward, going on the offensive. He kept his voice low, confident, certain of his actions. "Pribus, I need to earn her confidence if I'm going to figure out what Alicia's got planned. And that means that I have to show up to these meetings - meetings which, I'll point out, she'd have with or without me, and where my presence hasn't influenced it in any way."

Pribus grunted, but Tanner kept on pushing. "I need to find the perfect way to kill this bill so that the Republicans can't be held responsible. You told me that yourself, at our last meeting. As much heat as you might be receiving right now, can you imagine how much more anger will be directed at you if the bill dies - and it looks like the

Republicans were the ones to stab it to death?"

He saw Pribus grimace at that, and knew that he'd hit a nerve. "Trust me," Tanner finished. "This is under control."

For a long second, Pribus just closed his eyes, pressing his forehead against the knobs of his thumbs. When he opened them again, however, they looked sharply at Tanner. He frowned, not speaking.

"What?" Tanner finally asked. He knew that he was weakening his position by being the first to speak up and break the silence, but Pribus looked strangely suspicious.

"Alicia?" the head of the RNC repeated, raising his eyebrows.

"Senator Stone."

"And you're referring to her by her first name?"

A flash of concern, nearly panic, shot through Tanner's head. He struggled to keep his emotions in check, not reveal any hint of his uncertainty on his face. He hadn't meant to call Alicia by her first name, but after spending so much time with her, both in and out of the office, both clothed and naked… it just slipped out.

"Of course," he replied after a second, keeping his voice mild. "Keep in mind what I did to Senator Waltz?"

Pribus blinked, and then a grin slowly spread across his face. "Ah, the old honey trap."

"Honeypot," Tanner corrected.

"Whatever. I see - you're seducing her, getting some embarrassing footage so that you can threaten to leak it and expose her." Pribus grinned wider. "Both literally and figuratively, heh. That's the plan?"

"Yes," Tanner said shortly, hoping that his lie wouldn't be obvious.

Pribus's smile shrank a little. "She's not married, though, is she? No husband that you can threaten to address the pictures to, ruin the marriage?"

"No, not married." Tanner could see that Pribus

wasn't sold on this idea, and kept talking. "But that's the thing about being a woman in politics. it's a lot like being a woman in many of the other male-dominated fields; if something gets leaked, it always blows back much worse on a woman than on a man. A guy's caught banging a lobbyist, everyone shrugs. Bound to happen. But if a female politician is the one caught in another guy's bed, especially if she's young and attractive…"

"I see," Pribus mused. "You think that's going to be enough to bring this thing down?"

For a moment, Tanner forgot that Pribus was primarily focused on the education bill, not on the senator herself. "I'm not sure. That's why I'm sticking with her in all these meetings, hoping to find a way to kill the bill through a less… gray area."

It wasn't a gray area, of course. Trying to influence a senator with the threat of releasing illicit material was blackmail, a black and white crime, and Tanner didn't doubt for a second that, if he tried it on Alicia, she'd call his bluff. And she'd probably bad-mouth him to everyone as well, right away, trying to get out ahead of his story by putting her own spin on the situation.

Pribus still looked distracted, glancing down at the papers on his desk. Tanner sat across from him quietly for a minute, and then cleared his throat. "Actually, I was thinking."

"What?" A little bit of that previous flare-up of temper still danced around the edges of Pribus's expression, and Tanner nearly swallowed his words.

"Well, it's about this bill." He tried to fight the urge to fidget with his fingers. "Why do we need to kill it outright? This could be a great feather in the Republican cap, after all, if we just phrase it in the right way. We could show that we're progressive, pushing forward to help the American people despite a do-nothing president - and we could put some cost saving measures into the wording of the bill as well, to keep our constituents happy. This could carry a lot of pork barrel projects for our own."

Pribus blinked, opening and closing his mouth a couple of times before he spoke. "You want to pass the damn thing?" he repeated, as if Tanner had just suggested skewering and roasting a baby over a bonfire.

"I'm saying that there could be an opportunity here," Tanner tried again, but this time Pribus cut him off with a swipe of his hand.

"Not a chance. Listen, Tanner, I brought you in for one reason - to kill this thing. That's what we want, and that's what we're paying you to do."

"Yes, but-"

"No! No buts or anything else about it!" Pribus rose up a few inches in his seat, his anger back in full force. "You kill this bill, and soon, before it starts get into such a big media sensation that we can't let it just fade into obscurity! Either you kill this thing, or else you're fired!"

"Come on, Pribus," Tanner said, startled a little by this vehemence from the man. Even on previous assignments where Tanner had trouble, Pribus had always been understanding. After all, politics wasn't a completely controllable game. Sometimes, everything could be aimed in the right direction, and still not succeed.

"No. Not this time." Pribus forced himself to take a deep breath, but his tone didn't grow more calm. If anything, that note of anger in his voice sharpened even further, a knife with an edge fine enough to split a hair. "This needs to happen. If you can't do this, we're going to need to start finding someone else - someone more reliable - to handle the jobs that come our way."

Tanner tried to open his mouth, but he didn't have any answer to this. He could see from Pribus's expression that the RNC head wasn't going to budge on this issue.

"Got it," he finally said, sitting back and holding his hands up, as if surrendering.

Pribus maintained the glare for another second, and then sighed as he forced the anger out of his system. "Look, just bring the bill down. Hell, if you can get this Stone woman out of politics entirely, I'll even double your bonus for it. She's got a lot of people riled up - and I'm not just talking about this bill. You know that lots of our big donors have their ear to the ground in regards to possible future elections."

"Sure," Tanner said, wondering where this was headed. Pribus got to listen in to some very high-level rumors, whispered conversations among people miles above Tanner's class.

"Well, apparently this bitch is the full package. Strong, confident, aggressive, but with the kind of candor that the voters like - and enough savvy to understand that she's got to reach across the aisle at some times, and denounce her opponents at others." Pribus shuddered. "And there are even a couple wild rumors that she might eventually be destined for the top of the whole anthill."

The presidency? "She's not even thirty yet!" Tanner burst out.

"Like I said, long way away. But the rumors are still there, and they're making our donors nervous. So the more we can do to shove her down, keep her out of sight until we can scrape up enough dirt to neutralize her, the better." Pribus pointed a finger across his desk. "And that's your job. Now, get out and do it."

There didn't seem to be anything else that he could say or do. "Yes, sir," Tanner said, standing up from his chair. Briefly, he wondered if he should throw in a salute before leaving, but decided that Pribus wouldn't appreciate the joke.

"How was it? Bad as your face suggests?" Charlie called out to Tanner as he stepped back into the lobby of the RNC's headquarters.

"Worse," Tanner replied, shaking his head.

The old guard chuckled. "Well, you certainly look it. I'd suggest getting a good stiff drink. You look a little pale."

"That," Tanner said, nodding to Charlie, "sounds like an amazing idea."

But he couldn't go out for a drink - not yet, at least. He still had a long day of meetings with Alicia, pretending to be supporting this education bill, lying to everyone about his true intentions. He had to go and smile at Alicia, flirt with her, talk about strategy and pretend to be on her side, pretend that he wanted her, when he was truly searching for her weakness so he could kill her career.

And worst of all, he knew that his act of wanting her was no act at all. Every time she smiled at him, whenever he caught a glimpse of the luscious, strong, firm lines of her body through her formal clothes, he felt his drive weaken and waver.

Maybe he couldn't make it through this truce, after all. He ought to just kill the bill now, somehow, even though he'd lose Alicia.

But to do it to her, to give up the sight of the woman, hot-eyed and sultry as she lay naked in bed waiting for him to try and summit her, claim her wildness for himself…

Tanner groaned, wishing more than ever that he hadn't ever taken this job, that he was just sitting at home with a drink, waiting for Pribus to call with his next assignment.

CHAPTER EIGHTEEN

"Sorry, what?"

Tanner blinked as he looked up at Alicia, sitting across the table from him in his apartment. His fork was still buried in the homemade lasagna that the two of them created earlier in the kitchen amid laughs, tossed handfuls of flour, and licking marinara sauce off of various digits.

"I said, you seem distracted." Alicia frowned, setting down her own fork on the side of her plate. "And you're barely eating. What's on your mind?"

She was observant. Tanner cursed that attribute, even as he admitted that it made her undeniably more attractive, the way that she listened to him and remembered all sorts of miniscule details. He quickly searched for some sort of answer that would satisfy her.

"Nothing much, just thinking about work," he replied. He picked up his fork, transferred his mouthful of lasagna into his mouth. He didn't taste the ground lamb, the blend of aged parmesan and fresh mozzarella cheeses, the marinara sauce that they'd spiced up with some finely chopped fresh herbs. He might as well have put a chunk of cardboard in his mouth. He chewed, swallowed the lump of mush.

Alicia sighed. "It does get to you sometimes, doesn't it?" she said quietly. "It's just my first year - not even the end of that - but I'm already hating that feeling of always having more to do. It's overwhelming, like the Sword of Damocles hanging above my head."

"Sword of what?"

"Sword of Damocles." Alicia raised her eyebrows when Tanner's face remained blank. "Well, look who needs to polish up on his ancient Greek history! There's a legend about a commoner who wanted to switch places with a Greek king, wanting to live in unparalleled luxury and wealth. The king agreed - but to properly simulate the danger and weight that lay on his every decision and movement, he hung a heavy sword above his throne, suspended by the thinnest possible thread. The commoner had to sit beneath that dangling blade, knowing that the slightest wrong movement could bring it down, ending his reign forever."

And she knew history, too. Smart and well-educated. Tanner sighed. "A sword above my head, about to come plunging down if I make the slightest wrong move. Sounds about right."

"The unseen cost of power," Alicia said, sounding as if she was quoting something. "It really does get to me. I don't know how some of these senators, like Reed, can happily spend twenty or thirty years in the Senate without having some sort of nervous breakdown."

"It gets easier over time, they tell me," Tanner offered. "There's only so many different situations. After long enough, you've seen it all, and you know how to respond. You just need to make it that far, and then you're golden."

"Silver might be a better comparison, considering his hair," Alicia joked, and Tanner laughed along with her. It felt good to laugh, to forget, even if only for a moment, about how he needed to betray this woman and ruin her future.

After a minute, Alicia stood up, reaching over to slide Tanner's plate away from him. "Hey," he objected half-heartedly.

She paused, frowning down at him. "I can tell that you're not hungry. I'll put it in your fridge, and you can take it out if you get the craving for a midnight snack."

Tanner watched her walk away, her hips twitching back and forth with each step of her bare feet across his hardwood floors. She'd found an ancient apron buried in one of the drawers in his kitchen, and insisted upon strapping it on. Tanner didn't tell her, but she looked amazing, a domestic goddess. The career woman, it seemed, was equally adept in the kitchen as in the Senate chambers.

Even with her just in the other room, he felt a physical sense of longing seize him. Even knowing that she was in his apartment made it feel a little warmer, a little more like home. He hadn't realized how empty it felt when he was alone until after Alicia started showing up.

Funny, that; even when he'd had other women over, usually a conquest or two who elected to stay the entire weekend to get the full Keegan Tanner experience, the apartment didn't feel any different. If anything, he looked forward to when the woman would depart, returning to him his blessed privacy.

But with Alicia around, the place didn't feel cramped. He suspected that she could walk in on him doing just about everything - jerking his dick to a Victoria's Secret catalogue, for example - and she'd just smile, shake her head in mild judgment, and then leave him to his own finish.

Actually, she'd probably get that sexy, aroused fire in her eyes and head over to help finish the job, insisting that she had a much better alternative to the pictures of flat, airbrushed women on the pages of that catalogue…

Despite his gloomy thoughts, Tanner felt a little surge of sexual hunger stirring in his loins. Damn the woman for somehow managing to seize full control of his genitalia, infiltrating his every fantasy! Even the allure of internet porn didn't hold a candle to the thought of Alicia, naked and hungry for him, wrapping her legs around him and gasping in his ear as her nails raked his back…

A minute later, Alicia returned, hands now free of plates. "So, what can I do to take your mind off of work?" she asked, a wicked little grin dancing around her lips. "A massage? A warm shower? Maybe you just want to lay down on your bed and let me rub your shoulders?"

Somehow, Tanner knew that such a suggestion, although innocent sounding on the surface, would quickly lead to other activities. "Not sure that I'll be able to stop thinking about work," he admitted. "Sometimes, I just have to let these thoughts work their course inside my head."

"I understand." Alicia tugged her chair over closer to him, sat down and rested her head on her hands as she peered up at him. She didn't say anything, her eyes just boring into him.

"What?" he asked after a minute, a little unnerved by her stare.

"You're a strange one, Tanner," she said after a minute. "Keegan Tanner. Even the name makes you sound like an ass."

"Gee, thanks."

"Don't give me that fake 'wounded innocence' act. You ought to be my worst enemy. A Republican fixer, with all sorts of devious rumors floating around about just how low you'll sink in order to accomplish your goals. Nothing proven, of course, and no one will outright admit to anything. But the silences are plenty suggestive. From the moment that I heard you wanted to meet with me, I knew that you wanted to destroy me."

"Not me personally," Tanner corrected. He knew it was a weak defense, but it had the small benefit of being true. "The Republican leadership are the ones who want you to go away. I'm just the tool they chose."

"Interesting choice of words," Alicia murmured, and Tanner winced as he realized that he'd just called himself a tool.

"Not my favorite label, but a fitting one - and I've been called worse," he said.

"And they probably still want me gone, don't they?"

For a moment, he considered lying, or even just not answering, but Alicia's big turquoise eyes drew the honest answer out of him. "Yes," he replied. "More than ever."

Alicia nodded. "I thought so." She waited another beat, just watching him. "What are you going to do?"

He really needed to change the topic. "I think I'm going to take you up on that offer of a massage," Tanner said, standing up from his seat at the table. He tried to put on his best rakish grin down at her. "And I think I know just where I want you to start."

Alicia smiled back, but she just sat back in her chair, crossing her arms beneath her breasts. Tanner tried to ignore how the gesture pushed her tits up and towards him, failed utterly. "Not a chance in Hell, sexy."

"Tease," he said, no heat in his voice. He reached down, and after a second, Alicia allowed him to take her hand and draw him up to her feet in front of him.

"I don't know what you're going to choose to do," she said softly, standing in front of him, her head tilted back so she could gaze up into his eyes. "And I don't want to pressure you into anything. I'm not going to give you an ultimatum."

"Thanks," Tanner said, uncomfortable with the topic of conversation back on his crossed allegiances.

Alicia kept on looking up at him, her eyes seeming to look right through his shields and reducing his smokescreens to nothing more than dissipating mist. "But I hope you choose the right thing," she said, so quietly that he could barely hear the words. "This, what we have together… it's different. I think you feel it, too."

Tanner didn't say anything, as his brain and body fought bitterly against each other. He trembled slightly, hating himself.

"I think you do," she said again, so soft that his ears barely caught the murmur. She stepped forward to cross the last foot of distance between them, but didn't reach up to loop her arms around Tanner's neck and kiss him.

Instead, she just pressed her cheek against his cheek, hugging him softly.

Tanner stood there, frozen, for a moment. Her hair pressed up against his lips, his nose, and he couldn't help but inhale the scent of her, clean and floral and so unique that he knew that he'd never be able to forget it. His arms came up, slowly, almost jerkily, to wrap around Alicia and hug her back.

They stood there, arms around each other, not speaking, for several minutes. Tanner could feel the warmth of Alicia's breath through his shirt, splashing gently against his ribs. His need for her was like a physical force, bearing down with incredible pressure on his mind, trying to squeeze him flat.

But he resisted. Because as amazing as Alicia might be, he'd made a promise, and he had his duty.

She knew that he'd do his job. Even with her talk of a truce, of seeing through him, she had to know that he wouldn't be able to put off doing his job forever. He couldn't leave behind everything, give up his entire career, just because she managed to ensnare his heart.

Broken hearts could heal. Jobs, especially positions as powerful as his own, were a once in a lifetime chance. He'd never be able to reclaim this level of power if he turned his back on it now.

He felt Alicia's lips part. "Do you want me to stay tonight?" she whispered up at him.

He wanted her more than anything. His whole body ached for her. He knew that he'd have trouble falling asleep tonight, that he'd keep rolling over and wanting to feel her warm weight beside him. He wanted to lay in bed and spoon her, wrap his arms around her and feel her chest gently rise and fall as she slumbered.

"Yes," he said, the word coming out in a sigh of impossible sadness.

She nodded, as if he'd answered how she expected. "I think that you might need a bit of time on your own, to work through your decision," she said, her voice not unkind. She released her grip around him, took a step back. When she looked up at him, he saw tears shimmering in those big green-blue eyes, the sight like a dagger to his chest.

"You're going to go?"

Another nod. "But I believe in you, Keegan Tanner," she whispered. She leaned forward once again, and this time she did kiss him, as gentle as a feather's brush across his lips. "I believe that you're a good man, you'll make the right choice."

He nodded, fighting to hold back his own tears as he said goodbye to her, watched her catch a cab outside his apartment.

He stood at the window for several minutes, even after she left, wishing that he could see the ghostly afterimage of her, hear her voice in his ears again.

And then, finally turning away, he started digging through his own private files on various senators, figuring out which key positions he'd need to turn, subvert, in order to kill this education bill.

CHAPTER NINETEEN

"Hey Duecent, I'm taking a personal day. You're on the Senator for today."

Tanner rolled his eyes as he heard Duecent groan and gripe. The man really was a miserable excuse for a chief of staff. What kind of chief of staff didn't even get along with his own charge, wanted any excuse to get out of doing his work? The man ought to be demoted down to coffee run intern.

Still, Tanner wasn't too upset, because at least he'd been able to get ahold of Duecent when he called, instead of having a different staffer pick up the phone. Most of the staffers held about the same opinion of Duecent as Tanner, and they'd hand the phone off immediately to Alicia, instead of going through the chief of staff.

"Yes, I'm sure," Tanner reiterated after a second more of listening to Duecent's whining. "Look, this is your damn job. I've got other appointments and meetings to attend to. If you can't step in and run your own senator's campaign for a single day, well, she ought to fire your ass and ship you straight back to whatever hobo camp in Colorado she searched to first find you."

This, of course, set off a whole new tirade from Duecent. Tanner listened for a few seconds, established that there wasn't anything of importance in the rant, and then hung up on him.

There. Now, at least, Alicia wouldn't be wondering why he wasn't around. Tanner gulped down the last of his espresso, tossed the cup in his sink to deal with later, and turned to his laptop, sitting on his dining table.

He had a list of names, about half a dozen different senators. These, Tanner knew, were the men he'd need to flip in order to kill Alicia's education bill.

He barely got any sleep last night, but that was okay, because he'd put the wakefulness to good use in working on this list. These half a dozen senators sat on enough committees, held enough influence and seniority, to convince most of their peers to fall in line and vote the same way.

And furthermore, Tanner knew that he could convince every name on his list.

Some of them would agree right away with him. These were the dyed in the wool Republicans, those who put fiscal responsibility up on a pillar and knelt down to worship it. They'd likely oppose the education bill anyway, if left to their own devices, just because of the potential cost to the American taxpayer. Still, Alicia had talked about converting some of them by offering them projects specific to their state, and Tanner needed to make sure that they didn't rise to the bait.

Others on his list would prove more difficult. Some of these were staunch Democrats, ones that Tanner had crossed paths with in the past. Fortunately for his side, he still had much of the material he'd used to originally convince these senators to take his side - and he suspected that, in exchange for a promise to destroy the copies he held, they'd be willing to compromise their integrity for this bill.

If all else failed, Tanner could always fall back on the old trick of convincing a senator that he already had enough support to kill the bill. If there was one thing that senators hated to do in their voting record, it was to show a track record of supporting failed legislation. If the bill was already dead, there wasn't much of a reason for them to still try and support it by voting in favor - and it lent more material to their opponents when they next ran for re-election.

Tanner didn't doubt that he'd be able to convince every name on his list to turn his vote against this education bill. He still hesitated, however, knowing the true hidden cost of carrying out his visits to their offices.

If he killed this bill, that put his relationship with Alicia in the ground. She'd never forgive him, likely refuse to ever see him again - except perhaps to splatter him against the windshield of his car, he thought with a twinge of black humor.

But he didn't have any other choice. His whole future was riding on how this bill turned out, on seeing it fail.

He had to carry out his duty.

Tanner emailed the list to himself so he could pull it up on his phone, even though he'd already committed the names to memory. He left his apartment, striding off to Capitol Hill, off to go make the first of his meetings.

Meeting by meeting, Tanner worked his way through the day. He tossed back several more coffees in order to keep up his energy, using the caffeine to fight off the growing sadness that kept creeping into his chest. His heart felt like a stone, but he kept a broad and confident smile on his face, assuring the senators that he knew what their best course of action for the future would be.

One by one, he counted up the votes against Alicia's education bill. Some of the senators promised that they could also sway others in their voting bloc; others made no such promises, but Tanner knew that they'd exert an influence nonetheless. In some of his later meetings, he even dropped the names of senators from early meetings as evidence that this bill was destined to fail. Find one crack, apply the right pressure, and it could be widened until the entire institution came crumbling down.

It wasn't until Tanner's last meeting of the day that the man across the desk from him, Senator Vinter, brought up the point that Tanner had been hoping desperately to avoid.

"See, Tanner, I'm inclined to listen to you," the Louisiana Senator said, leaning back in his chair and linking his fingers behind his head. "I know that, most of the time when you happen to show up in my office, you talk good sense."

"Thank you," Tanner replied, sensing a "but" coming next.

"But see, here's the thing," Vinter went on, just as Tanner had anticipated. "Weren't you just in here a few days ago with that cute little thing-" the senator pronounced it as 'thang', "-arguing for the opposite point? Wantin' me to vote for this bill instead?"

Tanner took a breath, telling himself that he'd been expecting this question all day. "Indeed, yes, I was," he answered, not pausing to give Vinter a chance to dig further. "But this is all part of a larger plan. The bill needed to gain momentum before being brought crumbling back down." He sat back, hoping that Vinter wouldn't ask anything further.

No such luck. The furrow on the Senator's forehead grew deeper. "See, now, you've lost me. I might be just a simple Louisiana man-"

Tanner carefully kept his face blank. David Vinter was a lawyer with his own practice and had been previously employed as a professor of law. He was the furthest thing from a "simple Louisiana man" possible, despite the folksy image that his campaign advertisements - many of them partially funded by the RNC - conveyed.

"-but I'm not sure I really follow this twisted logic that you're trying to sell me on here." Vinter, still leaning back, looked expectantly at Tanner as he waited for a response.

"Of course, Senator," Tanner said as the wheels spun furiously in his brain. "See, the big target that we've got in sight isn't just this education bill, damaging as it would turn out. We've got our eyes set on a bigger goal."

"And what, pray tell, might that be?"

Inside his head, Tanner winced. Even though Alicia wasn't in earshot, saying these words aloud felt like a complete betrayal of her. He'd been hammering nails into her coffin all day, but this might be the final blow.

"Senator Stone, that 'cute little thing' you mentioned earlier," he answered, and sat back as the Senator digested this information.

"Ah, I think I see," Vinter exclaimed, the Deep South drawl in his voice growing a little thicker as he sat forward. "You're looking to show her up, aren't you? Get some egg on her face, is that it?"

"Yes, that's it precisely," Tanner nodded. "Brand new, barely even got her own office set up, and she's already looking to topple the whole anthill. We can't let her keep running rampant. Even if we kill this first bill, she'll have another, and another - a whole agenda. And I'm sure that you've heard the rumors about her."

Vinter, of course, hadn't heard any such rumors. If Tanner hadn't heard the rumors about Alicia Stone being a potential future presidential candidate, there's no way that they would have trickled all the way down to Vinter's ears. But Tanner knew that the man would hate the thought of appearing ignorant.

"Course, of course," VInter nodded, putting on an appallingly fake expression of knowing. Tanner wondered, not for the first time, how these dullards managed to keep on getting re-elected. "But just to be sure we're on the same page-"

Tanner wasn't going to waste any more time on this. "If we don't want her to become a constant thorn in our side, we need to make sure that she doesn't pull off a big platform, especially in her first term," he repeated forcefully. "And that's why I need your promise that, when this education bill comes to the floor, you'll stand up firmly in opposition."

Tanner carefully didn't mention any sort of threat. He didn't suggest that the RNC might change the amount of money that it poured into Senator Vinter's re-election campaigns, depending upon how he chose to vote on this issue. He just smiled, kept his tone light and pleasant, and let the silence speak volumes for him.

"Right, naturally," Vinter quickly promised. Dullard or not, the man knew when he needed to say the right thing in order to not lose the support of the hand that fed him - or rather, fed his campaign and kept him here in cushy, comfortable Washington, DC, instead of sweltering back in the swamps of Louisiana.

"Good." Tanner pushed back his chair, stood up. Vinter also climbed to his feet, but Tanner saw a little furrow reappear on the man's forehead as he gave Tanner's hand a parting shake.

"I gather that Little Miss Stone isn't going to take this well, is she?" he chuckled. "Thinkin' that she's got all this support, and then having it all pulled out from under her feet, like that magician's trick with the tablecloth and all the wine glasses. She's gonna be mighty steamed over this one."

Tanner felt a new dagger pierce his heart at the man's words. Alicia would be more than just steamed; she'd be crushed. She'd gotten the support from so many, promises, and she'd quickly find out that all of those words weren't worth the air used to shape them.

Fighting to keep his face blank and neutral might have

been one of the hardest things he'd ever done.

"Afraid that's just the way that Washington works," he said blandly, giving a little shrug with one shoulder. "She'll need to learn that, sooner rather than later."

"As we know, that's the truth," Vinter added, grinning with petty satisfaction at seeing one of his fellow Senators from across the aisle take a tumble. "Pity - but even if she doesn't get that re-election she needs, at least she'll have no shortage of job opportunities, with a cute little face and body like she's got!"

Tanner's hand tightened unconsciously into a fist, and he ached to just slug Vinter in the face, hard as he could manage. But instead, swallowing that bitter anger, he nodded, and headed out of the Senator's office.

There, he thought to himself, taking a moment to lean against the hallway of the Capitol building. That would be more than enough votes to kill the education bill.

He'd done his job. Simple as that. No need to even work outside of the system; he just called in the favors that others owed him, put on a little bit of pressure when necessary, and achieved his objective in just a day.

The bill was set to be called to a vote tomorrow. Tanner just had to wait for a little over twelve hours, watch the bill die on the floor of the Senate.

He needed, he resolved, to spend as much of the time between now and the vote as possible at someplace where he could keep a full glass of liquor in his hand.

Heart feeling like it was made of stone - and had just taken a direct hit from a sledgehammer - Tanner headed off to get drunk.

CHAPTER TWENTY

Tanner looked down at the drink in his hand, noting that he could still make out the details of the fractures in the ice cube, the little droplets of amber that clung to the inside of the smooth glass when he swirled the liquid. Grimacing, he threw the remaining contents back in a single gulp, gritting his teeth as the fiery liquid burned its passage down his throat.

"Another - and you'd best keep them coming," he called out to the waiter, not caring that she was halfway across the club's drinking room. Several other patrons turned and directed glares at him, but Tanner barely even noticed that he wasn't alone in the room.

He'd picked the American Tap Room, an upscale establishment that featured back-lit menus and plenty of wing-back leather chairs where someone could settle in and clear their thoughts, aided by the buzz from a good scotch or pub ale. The place was a big Republican hangout, but didn't usually attract the big hitters until later in the evening - just what Tanner wanted. He didn't intend to still be around by that point.

Arriving fairly early in the afternoon, he found the place still largely empty, and quickly dropped himself down into a chair. Two waiters had come buzzing over to take his order, and he sent each of them away with a request for scotch.

Pulling out his phone, Tanner sent a message to Freddie to tell him of his current location, although he doubted that Freddie would see that text for at least a couple of hours. Freddie's job tended to let him out late, one of the reasons why they met more often for drinks than for dinner.

Still, that would give Tanner a good head start on the drinking. By the time that Freddie showed up, Tanner intended to be at least wobbling on his feet, if not totally blitzed.

Of course, that would go quicker if these damn waiters would hurry up in keeping his drink full! Tanner leaned forward in his chair, pulling himself up with a hand on the arm of the leather seat. Where the hell was his next drink?

He shouldn't feel this irritable, he told himself - although the very thought only sent another spike of anger coursing through him. After all, he'd succeeded in his job.

Before starting to throw back gulps of scotch, Tanner made sure to dial Rich Pribus, passing on the news that the bill was going down in flames.

"And you're sure about this," Pribus demanded, his tone making the response more of a statement than a question. "Because if this thing passes-"

"Trust me, it won't," Tanner cut him off, sighing and not in the mood to be interrogated. "Look, I've got bipartisan opposition, from both sides of the aisle. Senior members on both sides. I know the right buttons to push to turn popular sentiment against a bill. The thing doesn't stand a snowball's chance in Hell."

"Well, good, assuming that nothing goes wrong," Pribus commented after another minute, still sounding a little nervous and not fully convinced of Tanner's skills. "I'll be watching tomorrow when this thing gets called up."

"Right," Tanner said absently, looking around for his drink.

Pribus paused for a moment, but didn't yet hang up. "Look, Tanner, this is good work, even if I've been putting pressure on you," he said in slightly gentler tones. "This is the kind of work that no one else can pull off, not nearly as well as you can handle it. We really appreciate this kind of help. I'll make sure that you're properly thanked for supporting us in this."

"Yeah, right," Tanner repeated, not really caring about whatever Pribus could do to thank him.

Another silence, just a little too long. "Tanner, if you don't mind my asking, what are your long-term plans?" Pribus finally asked.

"Long term plans?" Tanner repeated, sitting up a little as the waiter finally came over with his first drink. He threw it back fast enough to hand the empty glass off to the surprised man before he could leave, swinging one finger around the lip in a gesture for another.

"Yes. Ever thought about more of a leadership position? Something that's a little more removed from the dirty work, so to say?"

Tanner really hadn't devoted too much thought to his future, and especially didn't want to talk about it now. "Not particularly."

"Right." Pribus was definitely out of his depth here, but he kept on pushing forward. "Well, when you do want to have that conversation, think about a next step, you just let me know. There are plenty of spots in the RNC where I think that your talents could really help you out."

"Great." Before Pribus could try and act any more like a surrogate father figure, Tanner hung up, dropping the phone back into his pocket. Since he'd killed the education bill as Pribus requested, he wouldn't get much flak for hanging up on the head of the RNC.

And right now, he wanted to focus only on turning his brain off as quickly as possible, using alcohol to flip that switch.

The waiter came back a bit more rapidly this time with his refill, perhaps sensing that Tanner was serious about drinking - or, alternatively, sensing that he'd be able to collect a nice tip on a big bill if Tanner kept on slugging back scotch at this rate. Tanner accepted the glass, drank half of it, glared at the remainder.

Why did he feel so upset? Of course, he knew that the sting of losing Alicia would be painful at first. But he'd move past her, just like he'd done for dozens, maybe even hundreds of women. They came and went, always another one to make him forget about the previous, a parade of new bodies for him to conquer in his bed.

Aside from being the first Senator to climb into his bed, there wasn't anything special about Alicia. Sure, she had a tight body, but so did thousands of other girls. She wasn't the most well endowed girl, wasn't the skinniest, wasn't the shapeliest, and probably wasn't even the smartest - one time, Tanner had managed to convince a visiting Swedish particle physicist to peel off her panties and let him slip his cock inside her little trimmed blonde bush while on a weekend visit to DC from the United Nations building.

No, he insisted to himself, there wasn't anything special about Alicia. Sure, she'd seen through him from the very beginning, and her wry humor never failed to put a smile on his face. Sure, she fucked like a wildcat, with a sex drive that managed to keep pace with his own - a rare commodity among most women. He loved the way her eyes sparkled up at him, how those big turquoise irises could convey warmth, amusement, or raw sexual heat. Even now, closing his eyes, he could picture her lying in his bed, naked except for his bedsheet draped artfully around her curves, her eyes banked after their previous sexual session but still eager for him to come join her for round two…

Tanner growled at himself, shaking his head, nearly spilling his drink on himself. He needed to stop thinking about her, not dwell on all the nights that they'd spent together! All of this obsessing wasn't going to help him move past her.

In fact, it was probably making things worse. Even now, if he closed his eyes, he could almost convince himself that he heard her voice from the entrance to the American Tap Room, over his shoulder…

Wait. That wasn't just his imagination.

Tanner sat up in shock, this time not managing to keep his drink from slopping over the side and splashing across one knee of his suit as he craned around. Sure enough, he wasn't having some sort of bad dream - there was Alicia, standing just inside of the entrance to the restaurant and looking around expectantly!

Quickly, Tanner tried to throw himself back in his chair. He prayed that the tall back of the winged armchair would shield him. A moment later, he heard footsteps behind him, approaching, but didn't let himself turn around.

"Tanner?"

Shit. God fucking dammit. Tanner swallowed, tried to take a deep breath, coughed instead as the air didn't manage to make it down his windpipe. He sat forward, and Alicia's hand patted him on the back between his shoulder blades.

"Tanner, are you alright? Just try and breathe."

After a minute, he managed to draw in a deep breath, letting it out slowly. "Alicia?" he asked, turning and looking up at her beautiful, concerned face. "What are you doing here?"

"What am I doing here? You texted me," she answered, frowning a little deeper at him.

What? "I didn't," he protested, reaching for his pocket.

"Yes, you did," she insisted. She waited, rolling her eyes mildly at him as he unlocked his phone. Sure enough, Tanner saw with a surge of horrified embarrassment that, instead of sending a text to Freddie with his location, he'd instead sent it to Alicia's number!

"Oh. Shit."

"Not sure why you're so set on getting drunk so quickly," Alicia said, pushing his feet gently off of the ottoman in front of the armchair and sitting down delicately on the cushion instead. "But I was sitting around the office, Duecent was harping on me about something, and I figured that hey, there's nothing more I can do for my education bill tonight. Honestly, we've done just about everything that we can, haven't we?"

"Uh huh," Tanner nodded, grunting as an invisible knife twisted in his guts, reminding him that he'd betrayed this woman just hours earlier. He retrieved his drink from her hand, swallowed the rest of it. The attentive waiter immediately darted forward to take the empty glass from his fingers.

"So I thought that I might as well come enjoy a drink as well," Alicia went on. "Maybe it's a bit of a jinx to think about celebrating before the bill's been called to the floor, but I think that I've earned it." She smiled at Tanner, a smile that sent another crack lancing through his already shattered heart. "Who would have guessed that being a senator could be so exhausting?"

"You didn't notice the white hair on all your peers?" he replied, his mouth operating on autopilot as his brain tried to squeeze itself to death and his heart slowly fractured further. "It's not that they're all old - they've just picked up twenty years in the last decade from trying to please the American public!"

Alicia laughed, high and clear and agonizing. "It does

make a horrible kind of sense, doesn't it? Anyway, let me go get a drink from the bar, and I'll be right back."

"I'll be right here," Tanner called after her, unable to resist plunging another knife into himself by watching her cute ass swing back and forth as she walked away. She wasn't the hottest woman in the world, he tried to remind himself.

But the words didn't mean much when he wanted her desperately, more than any other he could imagine.

Tanner's waiter showed back up, fresh scotch in hand. "I brought you a double," the man disclosed, instantly earning himself another ten percent on top of his tip in Tanner's mind.

"Thanks." Tanner swallowed a big slug, not even tasting the complex flavors of the scotch. His mouth still felt dry as ashes. "Keep them coming."

The waiter nodded, and Tanner tried to paste his fake smile back on as Alicia turned and smiled back at him, giving him a little wave from the bar. His heart ached, broke, came back together only to shatter once again.

And it was at that moment, looking at this infuriating woman who wouldn't get out of his mind, that Tanner knew beyond a doubt that he'd made a terrible mistake.

CHAPTER TWENTY-ONE

The rest of the evening flew by in a haze of smiles on the outside, matched by Tanner's growing self-loathing and hatred inside his own head.

Somehow, Tanner managed to keep up a happy appearance for Alicia. He matched the female senator's happy tone, trying his best to keep the conversation away from talk of the education bill that would come up for a vote the following morning. Thankfully, Alicia also didn't want to spend the whole night talking about the bill, and he managed to keep most of the conversation on lighter topics.

Even with other topics of conversation, however, Tanner kept feeling the agonizing pain growing inside his chest, eating away at him from the inside. He smiled at Alicia, matched her flirty comments, leaned in as she ran her hand over his leg, while repeating to himself that he was absolute scum. He needed to just tell her the truth, break it to her before she discovered the full extent of his betrayal tomorrow.

He tried, several times, to summon up the courage to come clean. But each time he opened his mouth, he looked at Alicia, felt his heart break again, and knew that he was too much of a spineless coward to do it.

What the hell was his problem? He'd broken up with dozens of girls before Alicia, some of them with incredible callousness. None of them ever so much as disturbed his sleep the next night.

But none of them were Alicia.

"Hey," the woman said, cutting into his anguished thoughts. "What's going on with you? Your thoughts are all tied up with something, and it's not me."

"Right. Sorry." Tanner shook his head, wishing that she'd stop smiling at him, stop looking at him like he was the most special person in the world. "I guess my mind's just distracted. Maybe I ought to call it an early night."

"You sure it's not the dozen shots that you've put away?" Alicia asked, her eyes dipping to his glass, once again almost empty (Tanner caught a glimpse of his waiter, hovering on the periphery and ready to lift the glass out of his fingers as soon as he took the last gulp). "I didn't see how much you had before I got here, but if I had all that alcohol inside my body right now, you'd have to drag me home by slinging me over your shoulder."

"Yeah, it's probably the booze," Tanner said, glad of the excuse. He swallowed the last bit of liquid and handed his credit card off to the waiter when he stepped forward. "Just add thirty percent on for yourself," he added to the man, who nodded with a growing smile.

"Generous," Alicia grinned at him. She reached down and caught at his hand, tugging him up from the chair. Tanner staggered on his feet, the scotch making his vision spin and blur, and she quickly ducked forward to help hold him up. "Easy, now."

"I should probably go home alone," Tanner groaned out, but Alicia just ignored these words as she walked him towards the door.

"Nonsense," she insisted, as the waiter returned and

accepted Tanner's illegible scrawl across the bottom of the receipt before passing back his black card. "You'll probably not even make it up to your apartment if I let you go off alone. Trust me, I'm used to caring for drunken idiots - you should have seen some of my brothers, growing up."

"Brothers?" he repeated, feeling like the entire conversation was out of his control.

She nodded. "Two older ones. Three and six years older, respectively. They used to show up at my college dorm room, wasted off their asses, and crash on my couch and floor. I got really good at cleaning up after them." She smiled up at him, as Tanner gloomily pictured how two large men might show up and beat him into a pulp after they found out how he betrayed their younger sister.

Outside, Alicia called a car and bundled a still-protesting Tanner into the backseat. Leaning forward, she gave the driver Tanner's address, and then curled up against him, nestling into the crook of his arm as the car pulled away from the curb.

Back at his apartment, Alicia once again easily resisted Tanner's efforts to convince her to go home, that he had everything under control. "I'm not going to be able to fall asleep tonight anyway, thinking about the bill's vote tomorrow," she told him, not seeing him wince in the darkness outside his building. "And I'm sure that you feel the same way. So we might as well not sleep together, don't you think?"

Any other time, the idea of a girl - especially sexy, gorgeous, perfect, wonderful Alicia - practically dragging him into bed with free reign to do whatever he wanted to her would have seemed like a perfect fantasy. Tonight, it just stabbed another blade into Tanner's gut. Still, he couldn't manage to convince her otherwise, and instead watched with horror as she helped him up to his penthouse apartment. He felt a bit like he was having an out of body experience, stuck watching as his life came apart in slow motion.

"I need to talk to you," he finally managed to croak out as he sat, drunk and helpless, on his couch inside his apartment.

Alicia, standing up and wandering around looking at the scattered knickknacks on his shelves, glanced curiously over her shoulder at him. "Sure, go ahead. Going to tell me some of your history, now that I've revealed most of mine?"

"My history?" Tanner repeated, distracted and confused.

"Sure." Alicia picked up a picture of Tanner with a few of his college buddies, examined it, put it back on the shelf. "How'd you end up working as a fixer? For the Republicans, no less?"

Tanner grimaced. Maybe, he thought wildly to himself, he could drive her away if he gave her the real, unvarnished truth here. Then, the betrayal tomorrow would just be one more rock to add to the pile.

"They had more money, more desperation, and fewer morals," he answered honestly. "I majored in political science at Georgetown, didn't really pick a side at first. But I saw that, while all of the Democrats had these crazy ideals that wouldn't work in the real world unless every single person cooperated fairly, the Republicans were at least realistic about how fucked up everything was. I figured that, as long as there were some Republicans around, I'd need to be selfish if I wanted to get anything for myself. Might as well learn from the best."

"That's rather cynical," Alicia commented, but she was still listening, a little smile still flickering around the corners of her mouth.

He shrugged. "I figured that I wanted to be rich and powerful - who doesn't? If it meant that I had to fuck over a bunch of poor people to get it, well, that's how the world works." He knew that his words were harsh, cruel, but he kept going.

This time, his barbed insult flew true. He saw Alicia wince for a moment. "Well, cruel as it is, at least you're not trying to disguise it as help, like some of your comrades-"

"That's because they still need to pander to the idiots that keep on electing them," Tanner cut her off. He hated these words, hated saying them, even though they were all true. "I don't have that problem. This is how the real world works, anyway - people lie, cheat, cut all sorts of scammy deals in order to further their own ambitions. Even if it fucks over others, people that they love."

Another wince from her. "But you don't have to-"

"I lied." It came bursting out of him, louder than he intended.

He saw Alicia frown, not understanding. "Yes, I know. I saw through it, remember?"

"No, not that." He had to tell her. She deserved to know, even though it would hurt her more than he could imagine. "Tonight. Today. I wasn't out sick."

He waited, watching her face. He expected to see suspicion appear, her realization that he was still a liar, always a liar, that he could never be better than what he was. But instead, she kept on looking at him, still open, still trusting him. She believed in him, and he was about to destroy her using that belief.

"What were you doing?" she asked, her voice still not shaded by the hatred that he knew would come soon.

Here it came. "I was meeting with some of the Senators. I killed the education bill."

Nothing. She didn't believe him. He saw her eyes flick back and forth, trying to determine whether this was some sort of cruel, unfunny joke. He kept going.

"That was my job, Alicia. From the beginning. Richard Pribus, the head of the RNC, hired me to kill the education bill. To stop you. The Republicans are scared of you, and they wanted to shut down your agenda right away.

So they hired me, told me to find a way, any way, to make sure that this education bill didn't pass, without it looking like a purely Republican attack against American education."

Finally, it was starting to sink in. Her eyes held pain, now, betrayal even worse than he'd imagined. He plunged on, knowing that, as bad as this was, he had to say his piece.

"All of our time together - I was searching for weaknesses, ways to crack through your support. I did it today, the day before the bill goes to the floor of the Senate for a vote. I called in favors, leaned on Senators, didn't follow the rules. I killed it. It won't get nearly enough votes tomorrow to pass. Both Republicans and Democrats will vote against it."

Alicia sank down onto the chair across from the couch where he sat, her eyes brimming with tears. "No," she said, almost too quietly for him to hear.

"Alicia, I'm sorry," Tanner said wretchedly, knowing that the words were a band-aid slapped over a fatal wound. "I know that I broke the truce, that you didn't expect this-"

But she just looked back at him, and he hated the expression that he saw on her face. He'd been prepared for anger, sorrow, frustration, maybe even rage. He'd expected her to start throwing things, maybe wreck his apartment as she stormed out.

Instead, however, she looked disappointed, but not surprised. Almost as if-

"I should have expected this," she said, almost inaudibly. "I kept waiting for it, in the back of my head. A little part of me hoped that you'd be different, that I'd prove myself wrong."

She stood up, brushed at her knees as if dusting off a little bit of invisible dirt. "But I was right."

And that was it.

No yelling. No breaking things, no angry insults or accusations. Tanner almost wished that she'd yell, that she'd get her anger out, that she'd attack him for destroying what would have been the first big accomplishment of her career. A career that he had just confessed that he was doing his best to kill.

But Alicia didn't say anything. Not even goodbye. She just turned and slowly, almost emotionlessly, left his apartment. She didn't even slam the door behind her; it just closed softly, noiselessly, leaving no trace of her behind.

All that remained of her was the faintest trace of her perfume, floating in the air for a few seconds before dissipating.

Tanner didn't get up from the couch. His head still buzzed with the after-effects of the drinks he'd consumed earlier that evening, but he doubted that he could choke down another swallow. His stomach already roiled, angry at him, not understanding why this stress and self-hate had emerged so suddenly.

He finally grasped the sides of the sofa and hauled himself up to his feet - and then immediately sprinted for his bathroom. His stomach lurched, rejected its contents, and he barely made it to his knees in front of his toilet before the first heaves began.

Fitting, he thought darkly to himself as he purged the last couple of drinks from his system.

CHAPTER TWENTY-TWO

The next morning, the sunlight stabbed into Tanner's eyes like daggers, even through his closed eyelids. He turned and growled, trying to pull his pillow over his head to block out those rays - but the movement made his stomach heave, and he froze in place as he struggled to maintain control.

After the queasiness passed, at least for the moment, he slowly sat up, reaching up to wipe away some of the crustiness that clung to his eyelids. He felt like a similar crust had formed over his tongue, drying out his mouth and making him gag. He pulled himself up to his feet, swayed for a moment, and then staggered for the bathroom to scrub his tongue with his toothbrush.

After scraping his tongue off, he looked up into the mirror across from his sink. He scarcely recognized the face that stared back at him - pale, drawn, fine lines starting to betray his age. He tried to put on a smile, but it just made him look even more like he belonged in a coffin, front and center in a funeral ceremony.

"You're a dumbass," Tanner croaked to his reflection.

FIXER

The reflection just nodded, in full agreement.

He knew what he needed to do today. This morning - in just a couple of hours, in fact - the Senate would meet, and the vote for the American Quality Education Bill would be called. There would be some discussion, most of it pointing out issues with the bill, why everyone should vote against it.

Alicia Stone, of course, would do her best to mount a strong defense of the bill, arguing for why it was not only advisable, but necessary for America to improve the quality of education that it offered.

It wouldn't be enough. Speeches made great sound bites for the news networks to play that evening, but just about every Senator in the chamber would have already made up his or her mind - either based off of their own beliefs, what a more senior member instructed them to think, or based off of the corporation that helped fill their campaign war chest coffers. Her speech would earn applause from everyone - and change the minds of no one.

And then, just as Tanner wanted, the bill would die, failing to be passed.

He'd earn his pay, keep on maintaining his extravagant lifestyle, his luxury apartment, his oversized bank account balance, keep his memberships to all of the elite Republican clubs and keep on paying off the big bar tabs he racked up at them. He'd once again prove that he was the best fixer the RNC owned, that he could pull off political feats unmatched by the efforts of anyone else.

Still staring into the eyes of his wan and haggard reflection as it stared back at him, Tanner couldn't even begin to feel the slightest bit of pride in his accomplishment.

He got dressed, did his best to fix his appearance. He shaved off the stubble that coated his cheeks and jawline, but his lack of focus added several little cuts to his features. He cursed and blotted them with tissue paper.

Tanner looked through his walk-in closet, trying to decide between all of the identical appearing suits. Eventually, he grabbed one at random. Despite being individually tailored for his body, at great expense, it felt loose on him. He tied the necktie, tugged it roughly into place, and then left the apartment.

He'd woken up late, and the speeches by various Senators were already well underway by the time that he stepped into the visitor's gallery. Mounted on the upper floor and overlooking the Senate chambers, Tanner at least felt like he could hide in the back of the visitors area, avoid being spotted by anyone downstairs.

But then, just as he started to relax in one of the seats towards the rear, he heard a high, strong voice cut through the dim chatter in the chamber.

Alicia's voice.

As if pulled by invisible puppeteer's strings, Tanner leaned forward. Sure enough, he saw Alicia, standing tall and defiant behind the podium, her eyes roving out over the assembled senators in the chamber.

"We need this bill," she insisted, blinking. Tanner peered closer, and sure enough, there were tiny tears glimmering at the corners of her eyes. "Please, I beg of you, take a moment and put personal politics aside. There are many little petty fights that are always in play here, but this is a bill that transcends those quarrels. Don't think about your party, or your own personal agenda, or how this bill might not contain a project for your district.

"Instead," she continued, her hands gripping the side of the podium so tightly that her knuckles were almost pure white, "think about what this can do for our future. For our future as a nation, for our children. Schools all across the country cry out desperately for our help, and we have the power to do incalculable good for them. Please, please vote for this bill. Vote for a strong education for our children."

And then, before Tanner could pull back from where he leaned over the gallery, before he could retreat out of sight, Alicia looked up directly at him.

He couldn't take it. Clumsy, ignoring the murmurs of distaste from the other visitors sitting around him, Tanner dragged himself out of his seat. He staggered for the door, needing to get out, to get away.

Behind him, Tanner heard the Senate Majority Leader take the microphone, beginning the process of calling the bill to a vote. He knew that he ought to stick around and make sure that the bill didn't pass, but he couldn't bear to be here for even a second longer.

As soon as he'd locked eyes with Alicia, he'd felt his heart break anew in his chest, and he knew, beyond the shadow of a doubt, what he'd lost.

He loved her.

That realization slammed into him like a sledgehammer to the chest, nearly stopping his heart from beating. The physical force of that realization propelled him up out of his seat, halfway to the exit from the visitors viewing area, before he even realized that he was moving. He managed to get out into the hallway, where he slumped over, his head pressing against the cool stone of the wall.

He loved her. Almost like a blind man exploring an open wound, Tanner mentally explored this realization, sitting like a stone in the middle of his brain. He didn't know how it had appeared, coming out of nowhere, but it sat there, solid as bedrock.

He loved her. This wasn't lust, wasn't just a crush, wasn't like any of his previous relationships. Tanner could practically hear Alicia's voice inside his head, laughing as she called him a dumbass, pointing out that he should have realized this earlier, back before-

-before he fucked it all up, before he lost her forever.

And when Alicia looked up at him, during that frozen moment of time in the Senate chamber, he'd seen in her eyes that she had loved him too, once. Now that he saw it, recognized it in himself, he knew that she'd loved him for longer than he'd realized, back when they were still together, from that moment that their bodies had first come together.

She'd loved him, and then he threw it all away, destroyed that love, stomped on it and reduced it to nothing by betraying her.

Still leaning against the wall, trying to even breathe normally, Tanner nearly jumped a foot in the air as his phone started buzzing. He pulled it out, held it to his ear, just breathing into the receiver.

"Tanner?" Pribus. "Hey, buddy, you there?"

"Yeah," Tanner ground out.

"Amazing! I don't know how you pulled it off, but you're still definitely the best. I'll admit, I had a bit of doubt about your success with this one. I know, I shouldn't have doubted your skills, but I'll confess that I did. And then you go and prove to me that you've still got it, why you deserve to be on my speed dial list." Pribus sounded ecstatic. He babbled on some more, but Tanner tuned out these words.

Finally, perhaps realizing that Tanner wasn't replying to any of his compliments and praise, Pribus stopped. "Hey, son, you okay? You haven't said anything for a while, now. I would have expected that you'd already be out celebrating!"

Tanner opened his mouth, not sure what would come out. "Pribus, I need a break."

"Hey, of course! What are you thinking? Mexico? Maybe Vietnam? You know, the RNC has a private jet that we keep sitting around, all fueled up and ready to go, but I'm pretty sure that it's sitting idle at the moment. I've heard some great things about Spain, really cheap right now, and the girls are to die for-"

"Not a vacation," Tanner cut him off. "I'm taking a

break from working for you. From doing these jobs."

"These jobs?"

"Politics. Fixing things. Chasing the party's goals, just crushing whatever innovation people want because it doesn't sit with your own greedy ideals," Tanner spat out, anger bubbling through his veins. He straightened up from where he'd been slumping against the wall, his voice climbing in volume. A couple other visitors, exiting from the Senate chamber and wearing disappointed expressions (apparently, they'd been rooting for the education bill to pass) glared at him but he just stared back until they dropped their gazes.

"Tanner, we have other goals to help-"

"No," he cut the other man off. "No more fixing things to go our way. No more forcing people to vote the way we want."

Pribus took a deep breath. "You know that the other side does this, too, don't you? This isn't just us. Everyone does this."

"But that doesn't make it right," Tanner said, so softly that he wasn't sure if Pribus even heard him.

Pribus stopped talking after that, however, and the silence stretched on, the phone's connection crackling a little as the heavy stone surroundings blocked some of the signal. At least, Tanner thought dimly to himself, the man didn't wheedle away at him, trying to convince him to change his mind.

Finally, Pribus cleared his throat, spoke up again. "Can I ask why?"

Tanner took a deep breath, let it out. "Because I just realized what this is costing me."

On the other end of the line, Pribus started to say something else, but Tanner hung up on him, not even listening. Dropping his phone back in his pocket, he turned and headed out of the Capitol, back to his apartment to pack.

He didn't know where he was going, but he couldn't stay here. Not with the memories of Alicia, the realization that he'd lost the best thing that had ever happened to him, all around him.

He'd go to the airport, decide there, he said to himself. He'd get on the first flight out of there, no matter where it might be headed. Alaska, maybe, or Washington or Oregon. Someplace far away, someplace that wouldn't ever bring him near Colorado, or Alicia, ever again.

He had enough money in his bank account to last him a while. He'd maybe find a new job, or just do nothing. He'd always wanted to work at a small business somewhere - he was shit at using his hands for anything coordinated, but perhaps he could serve as a manager. Or perhaps he ought to go into sales.

He was, after all, good with people. Black humor surfaced briefly in his mind. Even if people didn't want to be convinced, he seemed to always know the right buttons to push in order to manipulate them.

It destroyed relationships, friendships, but he got what he wanted.

Unless what he wanted was Alicia, to have that love back. Even still, his heart ached, burning for her, a burn that he somehow knew would never go away.

Tanner left the Capitol, headed home, started dumping clothes into his suitcase. He needed to leave.

CHAPTER TWENTY-THREE

"No, not even close. Come on, you can't be serious with this shit." Tanner threw the printed paper with the proposed speech he'd been reading down onto the desk of the gubernatorial candidate's head speechwriter. "Are you even trying?"

The speechwriter, a young man with a sparse resume that proudly touted a C average in college as his crowning achievement, blinked up at him. "What's wrong with it?"

"What's wrong-" Tanner cut himself off, fighting to swallow his anger. He'd been struggling with anger more recently, as of late. Stages of grief, he thought blackly to himself.

Instead, he turned the paper around so that the speechwriter could see, stabbing down with one finger at a particularly awful passage. Just to drive home the issues with this section of the speech, Tanner had circled the paragraph twice and then scrawled "NO" over it with a thick tipped red marker.

"This," he spat out through gritted teeth. "You're stating that the governor's going to embrace coal power.

That's wrong."

The speechwriter peered down at the paragraph, as if he didn't even remember his own writing, and then returned a weakly watered down version of Tanner's frown back up at him. "No, the governor told me to put that part in."

"What? Why the hell would he want that in there, when one of the biggest planks in his platform is environmental stewardship?"

"It's not just coal, it's clean coal," the speechwriter said, as if this explained everything.

Tanner opened his mouth, but closed it again after a minute of searching helplessly for words. "You ought to run for a political appointment yourself," he finally spat out, the worst insult he could conjure up. He snatched the speech draft off of the writer's desk and stormed in to talk to their candidate himself, as the young man sat back and grinned at the apparent compliment.

The governor sat behind his own desk in the campaign office, looking intently at something on his computer with his mouth hanging slightly open. At the sound of Tanner opening his office door and barging in, the man quickly snapped up, clicking furiously at something on his screen as his mouth snapped shut.

"Not interrupting anything, am I?" Tanner asked, trying to keep his disgust out of his voice.

"No, no, not at all," the governor replied. Derrick Scott wasn't anyone's idea of a perfect governor in terms of policy, but he did have a confident speaking voice and strong demeanor, which was enough to keep him appealing to voters. As long as everyone listened to the style of his speeches, and not the lack of substance, Tanner thought that he could manage to squeeze out a win for the man.

Of course, after he spent a few years in office and accomplished absolutely nothing, Tanner had already decided that he wouldn't pick up the phone when they called him back to lead the man's re-election campaign.

"Derrick, what's all this I hear about coal?" Tanner asked, dropping the half-written speech onto the man's desk.

Derrick smiled, although it was more of a nervous gesture than a confident one. His bald head, shaved and polished, gleamed like a cue ball. "Yeah, Keegan, I wanted to talk to you about that. See, I've been talking to some folks over in the energy sector who are looking to provide a whole bunch of Florida jobs, and they say-"

"It's Tanner," Tanner cut in.

Derrick frowned in incomprehension. "What?"

"Tanner. Not Keegan."

His frown deepened. "But that's your name, isn't it? I like to call people by their first names, put them at ease."

"It doesn't put me at ease," Tanner snapped back. He knew that, at least the old Keegan Tanner would never talk back to a candidate like this. The candidate needed to be kept happy, well-fed, and complacent, while he did the real heavy lifting behind the scenes. But as of late, he found himself hating Derrick, hating everything about the man. He had absolutely no morals, and his charisma was as shallow as a kid's backyard wading pool. Next to Alicia, the man was just a cheap sock puppet-

Tanner closed his eyes for a moment, wincing. He didn't want to think about her name. He'd spent the last two months trying to not picture her, not remember her, not realize how much he missed her and wanted her. He could move on. Just needed more time.

"Tanner," he said firmly, opening his eyes after taking a breath. "Call me Tanner."

"Well, if you insist," the governor allowed - another thing that Tanner hated about the man. He backed down at the slightest sign of confrontation. Great for Tanner to get his way in disputes, but Tanner couldn't be at the man's side every second - and it only took a few seconds for a lobbyist to change Derrick Scott's mind.

"Anyway, back to this coal thing," Tanner returned, tapping the speech now sitting on the governor's desk. "Look, you can't put this in there."

"But it's clean coal!" Derrick replied, as if this made it different. "And the energy people are telling me that it will bring jobs-"

"Derrick." Tanner fought the urge to reach up and rub his temples. "There's no such thing as clean coal. It's just buzzword bullshit made up to lie to voters. It's going to bring pollution, not jobs - come on, there's no coal here! This isn't West Virginia!"

"But they said it's clean-"

"Derrick, your whole platform is about stewardship, both for the budget and the environment. Bringing in coal plants will destroy your environmental credibility, and the cost to the state when the President finally implements those carbon taxes he's been threatening for years will destroy your fiscal plank as well. You can't put this in a speech."

Derrick Scott looked put out - no, worse than that, Tanner realized. The damn man was pouting! Like a little child! What was he, eight years old?

Tanner wasn't going to cave on this. He waited, glaring at the candidate and not bothering to hold back the disdain in his eyes.

"Fine," Derrick finally caved, just as Tanner knew that he would. Dear lord, the man was seriously scraping the bottom of the barrel in terms of electability. "But listen, maybe instead, we could talk to the energy people and convince them to instead bring some other jobs! They were saying all sorts of fun things about fracking-"

Keegan Tanner, in a rare twist, found himself speechless.

He turned around, ignoring as the gubernatorial candidate kept talking. "Oh, and Derrick," Tanner called over his shoulder.

"Oh, yes? What?"

"The framed picture on the wall behind you reflects your computer screen," Tanner said with a sigh. When he walked into the office, the man had been browsing the "casual encounters" section of Craigslist, several lurid pictures easily viewable in the reflection behind him.

"Oh. Shit. Look, I just clicked a link in my email, I didn't know that it would-"

Tanner slammed the office door behind him, cutting off the rest of the man's protests. He'd probably sink himself with a scandal before he even made it a year in office, he thought blackly to himself.

The whole thing was an exercise in futility. He had just wanted out of Washington, and although he'd told Pribus that he was done working as a fixer, the man wheedled him into taking this position down here, working a short term appointment to get Soon-To-Be-Governor Scott elected. Tanner figured that the extra cash would help offset his heavy drinking bills, and accepted the spot.

More recently, however, as Derrick Scott drove him crazy, Tanner found himself pushing the booze away. Instead, he started spending more and more time in the little hometown gym located a block away, grunting as he pushed his body to its limits, letting the physical exertion of lifting weights and running on the treadmills clear his mind of intrusive thoughts.

But no matter how much he exercised, how many stupid things Derrick Scott said to him, he couldn't keep Alicia fully out of his mind.

More and more, Tanner realized, he'd made the wrong choice, had kept on making wrong choices ever since the woman saw right through him. He should have known, right then, that there was something special about Alicia.

But instead, he assumed that she was plain, that she didn't matter, and that he could replace her in the future with another woman.

Now, however, women held no interest for Tanner. One of the campaign interns came on to him, a sexy blonde barely out of college but already showing off incredible growth in the upper torso, but Tanner barely even noticed. He turned down her offer to go out and get a drink, kept his eyes away from her expansive cleavage, and felt only relief when she finally, pouting and put out, set her sights on the head speechwriter instead.

What would he end up doing? Tanner couldn't decide, didn't have any answers for the questions in his head. He knew that he still wanted to work in politics - it was his life, his passion - but he couldn't keep doing things like this, helping a sleazeball like Derrick Scott get elected.

He heard some of Alicia's words echoing back to him: "...we need to do something that matters - not for us, but for our future…"

Tanner paused. He wasn't just hearing the words in his head, he realized. Instead, he heard them drifting in his ears! He blinked, looking around and snapping back to the present.

There! Someone had turned on a television in the main area of the campaign building, and, her head and torso displayed on the set of some talk show, was Senator Alicia Stone!

Tanner shoved aside a low-level staffer as he staggered over, his eyes locked on that television screen. "Turn it up!" he barked, not sure who he was addressing. Some flunky must have heard him and held the remote control, however, because the volume on the set rose until he could clearly hear Alicia's words.

"So, Senator Stone," said the host of the show, frowning. The camera panned over to him, and Tanner wanted to curse at the cameraman. Go back to Alicia! "You're introducing your education bill again, despite the strong opposition that it faced last time?"

Finally, the camera returned to Alicia, looking strong and defiant and composed, so good that Tanner wanted to reach out and try and touch her through the screen of the television. "Yes, that's correct," she replied simply.

"You don't fear that the same thing will happen as last time? This bill will go down in flames, and opponents will lambast you for targeting pipe dreams?"

Alicia, however, had a response ready to that. "Is it a pipe dream to want better education for our children, for our future?" she fired back, filled with fire and energy. Tanner watched, wishing that his candidate Derrick Scott could channel even a fraction of that seriousness, that conviction and passion. "I don't believe so. If that's the label that will be put on the rare politicians who step up and do something, instead of just sitting back and continuing to let our country slide, well, it's a label I'll be glad to wear."

"And how do you think your chances are for the bill's passage?" the host asked next, after taking a moment to recover from the energy of Alicia's response.

Alicia sighed, her eyes dipping down. "I wish that I could promise that it would pass, as I hope," she admitted, "but it's going to be a tough call. Last time, I thought that I had the votes, but the bill didn't end up coming through. This time, I feel like my fellow senators are even more jaded and reluctant to stick their necks out for change by voting for a bill like this one."

"Doesn't sound good for your bill's chances," the host admitted sympathetically.

But Alicia smiled back at him. "Well, last time I thought the bill would pass, and it failed. This time, I think the bill will fail, so I'm hoping that it will pass!"

"Sounds like Yogi Berra's kind of logic," the host chuckled, but he was laughing along with Alicia, not at her. Her undeniable charisma had already charmed him, won him over to her side. Tanner felt a pull of longing, deep in his gut.

But more importantly, he knew that, as it stood now, Alicia's bill wouldn't pass. No bill fared better when it was introduced for a second time.

This education bill, just like the first one, would founder and die-

-unless he helped.

In that moment, Tanner wasn't even thinking of winning Alicia back. But he knew that he owed her this, that this was his one chance to make right the injustice he'd caused, the sin that had weighed on him for the last two months.

"Hey, Derrick!" he shouted casually over his shoulder.

Derrick Scott stuck his bald head out of his office. "Yes, Keegan?"

"I quit. Your campaign's the political equivalent of a dumpster fire, and I hope you burn with it. Enjoy watching porn in your office until the funds run out."

And as every single staffer stared at him, their mouths hanging open, Tanner left to go catch the first available flight to Washington.

CHAPTER TWENTY-FOUR

Two days later, Alicia Stone sat on the floor of the Senate, fighting the urge to bite at her fingernails. It was an old habit, one that she'd suffered with as a child and fought against when she entered college. She'd weaned herself away from it, mostly by throwing herself instead into studying and typing, other things to keep her hands busy, but she still occasionally felt the urge to pop a nail into her mouth and bite down.

Her bill was next up. Funding Our Children in the United States - FOCUS. Talking about the bill on talk shows, she had realized that she needed a catchy name. That night, she spent an evening with a bottle of wine and a notepad, rearranging different combinations of words until she found a halfway decent acronym.

Unfortunately, despite all her work to drum up support, despite her upbeat tone with the reporters and on the press circuit, Alicia knew, with a sinking feeling in the pit of her stomach, that the bill didn't stand a chance of passing. Already, she was starting to hear talk from her home state of disappointed voters growing disillusioned with her. They were mentioning her campaign promise that, if she couldn't pass her platform, she wouldn't seek re-election.

To be honest with herself, Alicia thought, she probably would end up acquiescing to their wishes. After this bill failed - if it failed, she reminded herself, try to stay positive - she didn't have much more energy to stick around and watch other bills go nowhere.

The Senate Majority leader, a disagreeably mild man called McConnor who bore the unfortunate physical resemblance to a surprised turtle, pounded his gavel on the podium and cleared his soft voice. "And now, we turn to the next bill, Senate Bill 1672, the Funding Our Children in the United States."

Here it came. Even Alicia had been surprised by how vehemently the Republicans tore into her, from the moment that she let slip that she intended to try and pass her education bill a second time. If she didn't know better, she might have guessed that they were actually nervous that they wouldn't be able to bring it down a second time with their scummy tactics!

But this time, the Republicans ended up not needing to worry about resorting to underhanded tactics. After the first bill failed, they had ruled the airwaves and television channels, pointing to this bill as everything that was wrong with the government process, why Washington remained in gridlock. Nevermind that they had voted against the bill themselves - no one needed to focus on that minor detail. Instead, this was just a small symptom of the larger problem of young, inspired people trying to drag fresh ideas into the stodgy and dusty chamber of the Senate.

Duecent had tried to talk her out of it, Alicia thought miserably to herself as McConnor droned on, reading off the sponsors of the bill. That was a man with good self-preservation instincts, if lacking in a spine. He could sense which way the wind was blowing even before it started - a great skill for someone managing a campaign, but far less useful once his candidate won her election.

As soon as Duecent heard Alicia explain that she wanted to take another crack at education, he told her that it was suicide. He fretted over how this would hurt her in poll numbers, how this would affect popular opinion of her...

He thought about everything, in short, except how it could help America.

For just a second, sitting there in the Senate chambers, Alicia found herself thinking back to Keegan Tanner. Just for a moment, she let herself daydream, picture what would have happened if the man stuck with her, stayed on her side, didn't betray her.

The bill would have passed the first time, for one thing. Tanner probably would have been out of a job, that was true, but she immediately would have snapped him up. With Tanner, instead of Duecent, acting as her chief of staff, she couldn't imagine her office running as anything less than a well-oiled machine. He'd probably have half of her requests filled even before she could speak them aloud.

And then, knowing that he wasn't just her campaign manager, but also the man taking her home each night...

For the last two months, Alicia poured her energy into her professional work. Being a Senator didn't leave much time for dating, in any case - a fact that Alicia found herself appreciating. She didn't want to think about filling that gap, trying to find another man to step into the hole that Tanner left behind.

Sometimes, late at night after a little too much wine, Alicia found herself remembering how their bodies had come together, how well she slept with him lying beside her, his arm draped lazily over her, marking her as his. He understood her, cared for her, challenged and pushed her, in ways that no one else ever had.

And, she feared, in ways that no one else ever would.

In the dark of the night, in those moments, Alicia felt tears prickle at her cheeks. She knew, deep down, that she'd loved Tanner. She never told him, never put it out there, never knew if he felt the same way. But it was love, sure enough, and that little flame still occasionally flickered to life in her breast when she thought of him.

She knew that he wasn't in Washington any longer. A press release, a couple of months old now, mentioned that he was starting to work for the Scott campaign, down in Florida. It would be a good challenge for Tanner, Alicia remembered thinking. She'd heard plenty of rumors about Scott, almost none of them positive.

And with Tanner off in Florida, maybe, eventually, she'd figure out how to move on past him and forget about him. Maybe, eventually, the last little stubborn flicker of love in her chest would finally extinguish itself and die.

"And now, we'll call the vote. If you could direct your attention to casting a vote…"

Alicia reached out for the button on her desk. The Senate used an electronic system to collect the votes from its members; instead of waiting for her name to be called and verbally stating her vote, she could simply select "Yea" or "Nay" via the button on her desk, and her vote would be automatically cast, counted, and tabulated.

A large board in the Senate chambers, mounted on the back wall, displayed the vote counts. Alicia looked up at it, trying to steel herself to watch her second - and likely final - attempt at education reform die.

To her surprise, the numbers in support of the bill seemed higher than she'd expected. She saw significant opposition - already, more than a quarter of the Senators had voted against the bill - but this was almost tied with the number of votes in favor! Alicia found herself glued to that screen, unable to look away, her heart pounding in her throat.

Both numbers inched upward. This was going to be a

close vote! Around her, Alicia heard muttering from some of the other Senators as they also tuned in to the numbers, watching to see if the bill passed or failed.

And then, as Alicia held her breath, crossed her fingers, and prayed, she saw the number of votes for the bill pass the number of votes against it!

The bill was going to pass! And indeed, as she watched, the last few votes trickled in, almost entirely in the "For" column. Finally, with more than ninety Senators voting, the tally for the bill stood at 61 votes for the bill to pass, 33 against it.

Alicia stood up from her desk, still staring at the display as if fearing that this was some sort of joke. Her brain felt paralyzed, trapped, unable to think. This couldn't be happening, couldn't be real.

She turned and looked slowly around the chamber, her mouth hanging slightly open. This couldn't be real. She'd talked to most of the other senators, knew that they weren't going to vote for it. Most of them, sadly but firmly, told her to her face that the bill just wasn't strong enough to pass, especially after failing last time.

How could this have happened? It wasn't possible, didn't make sense.

Alicia didn't know what pulled her eyes upward, up from the floor of the chamber to the visitors' galleries that hung overhead, balconies on the second floor looking out over the proceedings. Inexplicably, her gaze rose up, moving to the middle visitors' balcony.

And there, impossible to miss, sat Keegan Tanner.

Even from across the room, Alicia knew him instantly. She saw the sweep of his hair, the strong features of his face in profile, even caught a glint from his eyes. He wore his classic black suit, although she caught a glimpse of blue at his neck - a blue tie, rather than a red one. His eyes were on the board displaying the results of the vote, and although the distance was too great for Alicia to know, she thought that she caught a flicker of a faint little smile on his face.

A moment later, however, he stood up and turned around, clearly intending to leave.

Alicia's body kicked into action without waiting for input from her mind. The next thing that she knew, she was flying forward, running out of the Senate chamber and sprinting towards the stairs that led up towards the visitors' galleries. She didn't know which exit Tanner might use to leave, but if she made it up there before he could pick one-

Her legs burned as she pounded up the stairs, her breath coming hard inside her chest. She rounded the corner, cursing these classy, professional outfits that didn't give her enough room to breathe, to move.

And there he was. Tanner stood in the hallway, still, as if waiting for her.

Alicia skidded to a stop, her shoes squeaking on the marble floors beneath her feet. Tanner looked up as she approached, and Alicia saw a complex mixture of emotions painted across his face: fear, sadness, regret - but also triumph, shining through the rest of the mix and turning up the corners of his lips, ever so slightly.

Broad, strong lips, the kind of lips that Alicia knew would deliver an amazing kiss. The lips that, try as she might, she hadn't been able to stop imagining, softly finding her own and pressing against her.

"Hi," she said.

As soon as those words left her mouth, she grimaced a little; what was she thinking? Hi? Like they'd only just seen each other a few days ago, like two months hadn't passed with no contact between them? Like she didn't remember how they separated because he betrayed her, crushed her chances of passing this bill back when it had been a slam dunk?

"Hi," he said back, a strangely unfamiliar tone in his voice. Was he nervous?

Silence reigned between them for a moment. Alicia felt her body betraying her, slowly drawing closer to him. She nodded towards the doors that led into the Senate chamber, trying to fight the heavy blanket of desire that strangled her ability to form sentences, to think clearly.

"That was you in there, wasn't it?" she asked.

His lips definitely turned up. God, she missed that smile. It really transformed his whole face, softening his hard lines and revealing his warmer side, the side that she'd only discovered after peeling back his shell, those hard shields he kept up in public.

"I don't know what you're talking about," he answered, knowing that she saw through his lie, knowing and not caring.

"I didn't stand a chance. I knew that I needed to pass that education bill, but I also knew I didn't have the votes. I went in there prepared to watch it die." Alicia paused, looking at him, fighting that fish hook in her stomach that pulled her towards him. "Why?"

"Again, I'm not sure what you're-"

"Oh, cut the crap," she snapped, the words leaping out of her before she could catch them back. Her eyes widened - she didn't mean to yell at him - but Tanner's smile grew wider, as if he'd been waiting for her to call him out on his bullshit.

"Because I needed to fix the mistakes I've made," he answered, taking another step towards her.

God, she wanted him. "And you think that's enough to fix them?" she asked, raising an eyebrow, trying not to let herself get drawn into those strong arms, let him pull her against his broad chest. "One vote is enough to make up for all the hurt you caused?"

He shook his head. "No. It's not nearly enough." For a minute, the smile left his face as his expression clouded - but his eyes refocused on her, and the smile bloomed again, brighter, like the sun coming out. "But it's a start. One step in the right direction."

"Okay, one step done." She really couldn't think. She wanted him so badly, ached for him to somehow say the right words to make it all better. She didn't know what those words could be, but she needed him to say them. "What next?"

Less than a foot between them. His smile grew softer, his chest rising as he took a deep breath.

"This," he said. "I love you, Alicia."

Everything around her seemed to freeze, the air crystallizing. What?

"I love you," he repeated. She'd asked that last question aloud, apparently. "I knew it months ago, but I was an idiot, threw it all away. I realized that I made the worst mistake of my life, and today was the first step to try and repair that damage. I know that you'll never forgive me, that I can't take back what I did, but I want to-"

"Oh, shut it," she whispered, and gave in to that tidal wave of desire crashing through her head.

She took the last step forward, closing the distance between them. His big, strong arms were around her, pulling her towards him, needing her, as she finally met those lips and kissed him.

CHAPTER TWENTY-FIVE

"How did you do it?"

The question slipped out of Alicia in two breaths, slightly muffled by the pillows around them. Tanner, also looking significantly out of breath as he lay beside her, thrashed his way up from the tangled sheets to peer down at her. "What?" he asked.

She repeated the question. Tanner's bare, brawny arms and shoulders threatened to distract her, but she could hold out for a few more minutes, she insisted to herself. After all, they'd already broken her dry spell - twice. She didn't need to be a total slut, just throwing herself at this man, over and over-

Scratch that. She wanted to do exactly that. As soon as Tanner answered, she said to herself, she'd jump his bones again.

There was a decent chance that she'd kill the man from pure sexual exhaustion, or at least temporarily cripple his ability to walk for a few days, but it was worth it.

Tanner, meanwhile, tried to assemble his thoughts. She wanted to ask him about politics now? While they both

lay naked in her apartment, still gasping as they rode out the aftershocks from their last shared orgasm?

Still, he tried to pull together a coherent answer.

"How did I get the votes?" he repeated the question back. "The same way that I killed the bill a few months ago. Talked to people, presented the bill in the right way to make them agree with it, called in a few favors."

"But if you got all of those people to see it as evil before, how could you get them all to flip and instead see it as good-"

He pulled her in closer, still marveling at how she fit so snugly in his arms, the tingle of her bare skin as it pressed against his own. "It's all about framing," he said. "You should know this, of all people - you're a politician!"

"A very new and inexperienced one, remember."

"Ah, that's true. I can see that I'll have to teach you a few things." He slid his hand down over the curve of her hip, and she needed no instruction to wiggle in closer against him. For a moment, he found himself very distracted from the conversation.

"But in any case," he managed after a second, "a lot of it is just playing up the strengths and talking down the weaknesses. Convince them that the bills are different enough to count, that the first one, although it failed, started the national conversation. Talk about new cost savings, even if they were in the previous bill as well. Point out how their vote on this bill, once it passes - and I promised them that it would pass - would be a great talking point in their reelection campaigns, how it would help them with some of the school and teachers' lobbies."

After a second, Alicia just shook her head. "I think I'm going to need to learn a lot from you," she said, her tone considering.

"So, does that mean that you want to keep me around? This isn't just a one-time thing?" Tanner kept his voice light, but he did wonder whether she'd considered any sort of plan past dragging him back to her apartment and ripping off his clothes.

Admittedly, he hadn't objected to any of that.

From the moment that she cut his monologue short in the Capitol building by kissing him, Alicia refused to let go of him. Even though several reporters spotted her and started shouting questions about how she felt, now that the FOCUS bill had passed, she refused to slow down.

"You really ought to go talk to the press," Tanner protested, as she dragged him out to her car.

"Later," she answered, giving his hand a squeeze.

Tanner opened his mouth to advise her to reconsider, but two things swayed him; first, he wasn't her campaign manager, so he didn't have any real platform to tell her how to act. And secondly, more importantly, he caught a glimpse of her round ass poking through those ridiculous slutty-secretary pencil skirts that she loved to wear, and his dick reached up to pin his tongue down in place. "Don't mess this up for me," it hissed at Tanner's brain, threatening to rip itself off and leave if he didn't keep silent.

Tanner kept silent - up until they were in Alicia's apartment, and she was attempting to climb him like a tree, her arms around him, her lips locked on his.

"Alicia, are you sure-" he began, but she leaned back, raising her eyebrows and frowning at him.

"You really want to talk, instead of having wild, crazy sex with a Senator?" she asked, pushing her chest forward to bump against him and scramble his brains even further.

Tanner's dick repeated its threat, but he still took a deep breath and held it at bay for a second. "Look, Alicia, I really do love you, even though we've been apart. I've been stuck with idiots, and all I could think was how much I screwed up by letting you go-"

She started to reach for his pants, but he had to make it through this. "I know that you probably don't trust me, but I'll do whatever it takes," he insisted, reaching down and catching her hands, pinning them inside his own. "Just tell me what you need-"

"Oh my god, and I thought that you were smart!" Alicia snapped at him.

His eyebrows shot up on his forehead. "Excuse me?"

She took a step back, planting her hands on her hips and jutting out her rack in a way that almost made Tanner go cross-eyed. "I love you too, you big, dumb idiot," she said, following this with a massive eye roll.

"Really? Your body language doesn't quite say it."

Alicia sighed, swept her hair back from her face - and then, right in front of Tanner, started peeling off her clothes, dropping each article delicately into a growing pile on the floor.

"Er, what..." He couldn't even finish the sentence, his eyes locked onto her body. How the hell had he ever let go of this one?

"You've got a choice," Alicia said, already down to just her bra and panties (a matching black lace set, Tanner couldn't stop from observing). "You can either come into my bedroom and let me show you exactly what I mean when I say that I love you and have been going crazy thinking about you, unable to get you out of my head for the last two months..."

"Or?" he managed to get out after her pause.

Alicia turned away, letting him see her fingers as they wandered up her back, found the strap to her bra, and popped it free. "Or you can keep standing out here, which seems like a clear rejection of the fact that I love you like crazy, even though you're a bit of a dense ass at times."

The bra slipped off of her crooked finger as she sauntered away from him, into the bedroom. Tanner's eyes locked onto her ass, barely concealed in those lacy black panties, lazily swinging back and forth.

He immediately made up his mind. He headed forward, chasing after her, unable to keep a wild, stupid smile from blooming on his face.

As soon as he stepped into the bedroom, he found Alicia filling his arms, warm and soft and floral, a sensory overload. She kissed at him, touched him like she couldn't get enough of his body, and helped his suddenly clumsy fingers remove the rest of his clothes.

They didn't even make it to the bed. Tanner dragged her down to the floor and she straddled him, riding him and feeling his hardness take her as she bent forward to kiss him, her breasts hanging and brushing against his muscled chest.

"And that's how much I love you," she whispered to him, after they'd both lost control, exploded, moaned and clutched at each other as they came together.

"That's all?" he cracked.

Her slow, sexy, hungry grin was all it took to encourage him to sweep her up and drop her on top of her bed. He landed astride her a second later, already kissing her first on the lips, and then using his tongue and hands to further explore her body.

Now, lying on the bed in the tangled aftermath of this second round, Tanner shifted, and felt something wobble in the bed beneath them. "We may have broken your bed," he said apologetically to Alicia.

She shrugged, the motion sending a delightful little quiver running down the length of her body. "I can get another one for next time," she replied.

After a second, Tanner propped himself up on one elbow. "And there's going to be a next time?" he asked, aware that he sounded a bit like a broken record. "You want to keep me around?"

Alicia blinked long eyelashes up at him, mesmerizing him with those blue-green eyes. He never wanted to forget this moment, never wanted it to end. "I love you," she said simply, her eyes proclaiming this honest truth. "Somehow, even though you're a total ass, you managed to get my heart. I'm yours."

Tanner bent forward and kissed her, blinking as he felt hot tears welling up in his eyes. "And I love you too, even though you're the most frustrating person I've ever encountered," he whispered back, trying to shake his head so that the tears didn't fall on her face.

They did, however, and mingled with her own. "Now you've got me crying, too, you idiot," she sobbed out, even as her arms clung to him. She pulled him close, holding onto him like a rock in a stormy sea. They both breathed deeply, trying to keep themselves under control.

They failed.

"There's tissues over there," Alicia finally sniffled out, and Tanner reached over to grab the whole box. He watched as she sat up and loudly blew her nose, smiling even as he wiped at his own cheeks.

"Well, I'm not sure that Pribus is going to give me my old job back," he said, trying to keep his fingers from reaching out to cup those incredible breasts that hung from Alicia's chest as she pitched her tissue towards the garbage.

She smiled a moment later, as his fingers curled around and gently squeezed her breasts against her ribcage. "Why's that matter?"

"Without a job, I'm probably going to be spending a lot of time living out of this apartment," he answered. "I sold my old place when I moved down to Florida. I wanted to make a clean break of things."

"Yeah, that worked out well," she snorted. "And I've got a job opportunity for you, anyway."

He leaned in behind her, kissed her neck. "What's that?"

"Well, you're the one who knows all about what I should or shouldn't be doing as an elected politician, right? Even though I hate to admit it, I could use your advice, your guidance on how to get my way with all these stuffy old men in Congress."

"This is true. So what are you suggesting?"

She turned her head so she could gaze back at him as he traced a line of kisses down her shoulder. "I think the position of Chief of Staff for my office is about to open up. What do you say?"

He paused, looking up at her. "You realize that you're suggesting that we be together practically twenty-four seven, don't you? And you're going to have a lot of arguments with me. Even though you'll eventually realize that I was right all along."

"Yeah, right," she sniffed. "But yes, I do realize what I'm asking of you."

For a long minute, Alicia watched as Tanner considered the idea. Even naked in bed with her, the gears in his head were turning, examining the offer from every angle. She loved watching his brain work like this, thinking through every possible scenario, weighing every single option.

"What's the dental plan like?" he finally asked.

Laughing, she spun around, intending to punch him. Instead, however, they ended up tangled together, flopping back down on the tortured bed, limbs intertwined and bodies pressed together.

"Is that a yes?" she asked, inches from his face.

He leaned in and kissed her. "Of course it is. I love you."

"I love you too," she answered, her heart singing, and she leaned in for another kiss, this one longer and deeper.

Afterwards, Tanner fought off the sheet that had somehow knotted itself around his leg, running a finger down his chest and noting the little beads of sweat that came together. "If you want any more sex out of me," he panted out, "I need to get some water into my system before I end up dying of dehydration."

"Ah, such an awful way to go," Alicia responded immediately, her eyes sparkling up at him as he fought his way out of bed. "And so instead, you're just going to leave me here alone? So naked, abandoned in this bed with no one else to help me pass the time…"

Despite all the activity of the last couple of hours, Tanner still felt his loins urge him to jump back into bed, to return for yet another round. With an effort, he pushed away that longing. Soon, he promised himself.

Duty called, first.

"Nope, you're not staying there, either," he told Alicia. "You're getting up, dressed, and then coming out to give a press conference on the success of the FOCUS bill. First task for you, as your new chief of staff, is to make sure to maximize the press attention for this."

He watched as Alicia rolled her eyes at him. The gesture made some other parts of her jiggle most appealingly, and he quickly averted his gaze before she dragged him back into bed yet again.

"Such a taskmaster," she sighed, climbing up. "I can see that we're going to have a lot of friction."

"And we'll find some way to resolve all that tension, I'm sure," Tanner murmured back, and saw Alicia blush before she turned away to get dressed.

And even as he ran through talking points in his head, mentally figuring out how to best prep Alicia for confronting the inevitable shouted questions from reporters, Tanner made sure to watch and enjoy the show as she shimmied back into her clothes.

CHAPTER TWENTY-SIX

"There's something different about you," Freddie said, frowning as he waggled his finger at Tanner. "I can't quite put my finger on what it is, but I know that something's off. Did you get your hair cut?"

"Try again," Alicia laughed from Tanner's other side before he could respond.

Freddie grinned briefly at her, looking past Tanner as if he wasn't even there, and then returned his attention back to his best friend. "No, I'm going to get this. Did you pick up yet another STD? I'm impressed that you haven't already caught them all."

"Okay, that's enough," Tanner groaned, as both Freddie and Alicia dissolved into giggles. "Yes, I'm out with Alicia, and the two of us are together. Officially."

"Finally," Alicia added, provoking another snort from Freddie.

Needing to change the topic, Tanner turned his attention back to Freddie. "How about you?" he asked. "You're still seeing that girl from earlier? Crystal? Christine?"

"Cristina, and sadly, I'm not," Freddie admitted glumly. "She wanted a guy who'd be out in the bars every night, and my liver threatened me, told me that I had to choose - either break up, or look for a transplant. I decided that I'd rather keep my internal organs than have a long-term girlfriend with drinking as her top interest."

Alicia sighed. "Too bad. We could have gone on some lovely double dates together."

Both of the men shared a private glance, rolling their eyes at each other. Freddie might like teasing Tanner about his new relationship status, but he knew that any sort of double date would end up with both of the women laughing and having a great time together, while both of the men just sat, drank, and waited for it to be over.

Still, Tanner's face brightened as he turned back to Alicia, loving the feel of her leaning in against him. Solid, comforting, soft and warm and supple. He couldn't wait to get her back to her apartment - although, already, the space was starting to feel a bit cramped.

He hadn't said anything to her, not yet - but Tanner had set up several alerts on property sites, waiting for something in the right neighborhood, at the right price, to pop up so he could pounce on it. A good redirection of his predatory political instincts, he figured.

Not that those instincts weren't still getting a workout, serving as Alicia's chief of staff. Tanner quickly discovered that he had the rare talent of spotting incoming attacks from political opponents before they landed - it came naturally to him, considering how he'd helped to spearhead so many of those attacks in the past. He knew just how to counter them, and the Republicans were finally starting to realize that the measures Alicia championed weren't just going to fade away from normal blocking attempts.

After the FOCUS bill's "miraculous" passage, Alicia quickly became a media darling. Her clear approach to speaking, her strong beliefs that radiated through in every speech she gave, and her quick wit and ever-present sense of humor made her an immediate favorite on talk shows, and she appeared on several national programs, including The Daily Show (a personal favorite of Tanner's, and he nearly fainted when Alicia invited him to come along and meet the host before the actual taping of the show). After the bill faded from the news, Alicia stopped receiving quite as many calls for quotes on various topics - but Tanner made sure to collect the personal contact information of many of the reporters and television show producers, gathering ammunition for the next battle that Alicia set out to fight.

And he knew that Alicia had an entire list of other social issues and important bills that she wanted to champion.

Even tonight, although Alicia was now laughing and enjoying her drink as she chatted back and forth lightly with Freddie, Tanner had been forced to practically drag her away from the review of a bill she'd been asked to consider co-sponsoring. "No more work!" he had insisted, laughing as she comically tried to clutch the sofa where she'd been sitting. "Come out and play!"

"I don't wanna!" Alicia cried back, even as tears of laughter streaked down her cheeks and she fought to keep from collapsing into giggles at how Tanner was scooping her up. "All the other kids laugh at me and try to get me blackout drunk!"

"They're laughing with you, not at you!" Tanner countered, grunting as he finally managed to get her slung up and over his shoulder, like a bag of potatoes. "Think of this as a visit to your constituents!"

"My constituents are back in Colorado, you jerk," Alicia replied, but then fell silent. A moment later, Tanner jumped as a pair of hands grabbed his ass. "Hey, look at this! I found something?"

"What did you find?"

"A cute little butt!" Another pinch from her. "And I wonder what's on the other side…"

"Stop, hey!" Tanner groaned, as she wormed around, her hands diving under his clothes. "You're going to make me drop you!"

"Worth it!" came Alicia's muffled reply, as Tanner finally sagged back down on the couch, worried that he'd drop Alicia on her head and end up having to take the Senator to the hospital. She landed on his lap, grinning up at him as her hands spread to inappropriate areas.

"Plenty of time for that afterwards - we're going to be late to meet Freddie," Tanner protested, making a half-hearted effort to stand up.

"Oh well," Alicia replied, and then unzipped his pants.

Somehow, Tanner only remembering to zip up his pants as they stepped into the bar, they managed to only arrive about fifteen minutes past the time that they'd given Freddie.

"You know," Alicia now said, peering at Freddie, "I do know a couple of other nice young women who happen to be single at the moment. I could see about getting you a date, if you wanted!"

Freddie turned anguished eyes on Tanner. "This always happens," he moaned. "Oh, I'm not single, but I happen to have a single friend! Let me set you up? Do you know how many set-up dates I've been on?"

"Forty-eight," said Tanner, who had heard this speech before.

Freddie shook his head, his eyes drooping sadly. "It's forty-nine, now. My hairdresser tried to set me up with one of her friends. Her friend turned out to be forty-five and with a bee's nest of a hairdo so big that she probably had squirrels living in it."

"So what, no second date with her?"

"She offered," Freddie said with a deadpan face, "but I turned her down. She wanted to 'go out clubbing like those young folks do', and I was worried that her hair would end up devouring another victim."

"Shame," Tanner said, shaking his head.

"Well, this woman that I'm picturing for you is young, cute, and has normal sized hair," Alicia kept pressing. "Come on, maybe set-up number fifty will be the one that ends up working out!"

Freddie still looked doubtful, so Alicia changed her approach. "She also wears a size four dress, and a size D bra," she added.

Immediately, Tanner's buddy perked up. "Okay, maybe I deserve to give her a shot. After all, who am I to judge people before at least meeting them, right?"

Tanner turned and looked down at Alicia. "You're evil, you know that?" he told her. "Everyone always believes that the Republicans are evil, but I think that it's you, masterminding the whole thing."

She just smiled back at him, her blue-green eyes so full of warmth and life and love that he felt like he could happily drown in them. "Yeah, but you love me, so it's okay."

"I do love you, at that," he admitted, leaning in to kiss her.

"And I love you, so much," she whispered back after the kiss, not leaning back from his face, gazing into his eyes. "You drive me crazy, but you're also the smartest, most driven, most principled man I know. And I love you."

He kissed her again, feeling his heart sing, beating in time with hers. Even Freddie's groan was half-hearted, as if the man, despite acting like a curmudgeon, knew that he was seeing Tanner happier than he'd ever felt before.

For the first time in his life, Tanner didn't feel focused on the present, afraid to consider what might come next in the future. Until now, he'd always told himself that he needed to live in the moment, not think about where he'd be headed next, what was in store for him in the future.

After all, for most politicians, there was little reason to ever look further ahead than the next election cycle.

But now, he wanted to stare forward into his bright future until he went blind. Even now, just sitting with his arm wrapped around Alicia, Tanner couldn't wait for the next step. Getting a house, maybe secretly lifting one of Alicia's rings to get her finger's size and then visiting a few jewelry shops, looking for that perfect diamond...

Yes, he couldn't wait for the future.

Briefly, Tanner wondered if Alicia had any idea what he might be considering for the future. She hadn't said anything, certainly, hadn't given him any sort of hint or prodding. But still, when he sometimes looked up to find her just gazing at him, loving him, the strength of her affection for him so strong that he could practically feel it as a physical thickening in the air, he suspected that she knew a lot more about what he was considering than what she was willing to divulge.

Not that he minded. Tanner knew that Alicia was smarter than him - one of the first times he'd realized that about his dating partner, and found comfort in it.

Right now, he could just relax, focus on helping her as much as he could, and wait for that bright future to arrive.

Tanner realized that he'd been tuning out for a few minutes, and quickly played back the last bit of conversation between Freddie and Alicia in his head. They'd been talking in incomprehensible jargon about some sort of computer security stuff; Alicia had a cybersecurity bill sitting on her desk, waiting to be reviewed, and Freddie clearly had some strong feelings on the matter.

He listened idly, focusing more on watching the animation, the energy, in Alicia's face and hands as she debated with Freddie. This woman, he thought fondly, would go far in politics. For once, he found himself believing the hype that the pundits summoned up when they debated who they'd see as contenders in future

Presidential campaigns.

And Tanner swore, yet again, to himself that he was done with tearing people down. He'd left that part of himself behind. Now, instead of focusing on holding back others, he was going to help make things happen, make a brighter future.

After all, he considered happily for a moment before crushing the thought as too much, too soon, that future might not belong just to Alicia and himself.

Who knew what their future might hold?

No matter what, however, Tanner knew that he'd be spending the rest of his life working to make sure that Alicia was happy, as happy as he could promise her. He loved her, and he wanted to spend the rest of his life showing her, each and every day.

So he sat next to his true love and his best friend in the Capitol Lounge, sipping his drink and listening to them talk, enjoying being happy. This was all he needed.

THE END

ABOUT THE AUTHOR

Samantha Westlake has an unfortunate habit of staying up far too late, reading romance and saucy stories when she really should be sleeping and preparing for work. Samantha currently lives in San Francisco, CA. She draws her inspiration from the wonderful people of the city around her, and can often be found relaxing on the wharf, gazing out in the mornings as the fog burns off the bay.

Made in United States
Orlando, FL
10 April 2022